Ghos

The ghost was g
wasn't gliding no
dance, and every
double and shake with laughter. His thin
cackle was the sound Jimmy had heard.
Evidently he was enjoying the joke he had
played.

That made Jimmy crosser than ever. He
stuck his head farther around the door-
jamb and yelled 'Boo!' at the top of his
lungs. The ghost gave a thin shriek and
leaped two feet in the air, then collapsed on
the stairs.

As soon as Jimmy saw he could scare the
ghost even worse than the ghost could scare
him, he wasn't afraid any more and he came
right into the hall. The ghost was hanging
on the banister and panting. 'Oh, my
gracious!' he gasped. 'Oh, my goodness!
Boy, you can't do that to me!'

GHOSTLY LAUGHTER

Edited by Barbara Ireson

Beaver Books

A Beaver Book
Published by Arrow Books Limited
62–5 Chandos Place, London WC2N 4NW

An imprint of Century Hutchinson Ltd

London Melbourne Sydney Auckland
Johannesburg and agencies throughout the world

First published 1981
Fourth impression 1986
Copyright © this collection Barbara Ireson 1981

Set in Garamond
Printed and bound in Great Britain by
Cox & Wyman Ltd, Reading

ISBN 0 09 941150 4

Contents

Acknowledgements

The author and publishers would like to thank the following people for giving permission to include in this anthology material which is their copyright.

Jonathan Cape Limited for the 'The Mysterious Barricades' by Joan Aiken from *All and More*

Curtis Brown Limited for 'The House That Lacked a Bogle' by Sorche Nic Leodhas from *Scottish Ghosts*

Catherine Gleason for 'The Gargoyle' by Roger Malisson

Victor Gollancz Limited for 'Sonata for Harp and Bicycle' by Joan Aiken from *A Bundle of Nerves*

Hamish Hamilton Limited for 'The Night the Ghost Got In' by James Thurber, from *Vintage Thurber* volume 2

The Hamlyn Publishing Group Limited for 'First Performance' from *The Obstinate Ghost* by Geoffrey Palmer and Noel Lloyd, originally published by Odhams Press Limited

Harcourt Brace Jovanovich, Inc., for 'The Spooky Thing' by William O. Steele, from *The Spooky Thing*

A. M. Heath & Company Limited for 'Jimmy Takes Vanishing Lessons' by Walter R. Brooks

Pamela Klacar for 'The Bungling Bunyip' by Pamela Vincent

Scott Meredith Literary Agency, Inc., for 'Me and My Shadow' by Eric Frank Russell, which is reprinted by permission of the author and the author's agents, Scott Meredith Literary Agency Inc., 845 Third Avenue, New York, New York 10022

Thames Television and Brian Pattern for 'The Man Who Hated Children', which appeared in *The Best of Shadows*, published by Carousel

Harvey Unna and Stephen Durbridge Limited for 'The Murderous Ghosts' by Rosemary Timperley

The Night the Ghost Got In

James Thurber

The ghost that got into our house on the night of 17
November 1915 raised such a hullabaloo of mis-
understandings that I am sorry I didn't just let it
keep on walking, and go to bed. Its advent caused
my mother to throw a shoe through a window of the
house next door and ended up with my grandfather
shooting a patrolman. I am sorry, therefore, as I
have said, that I ever paid any attention to the
footsteps.

They began about a quarter past one o'clock in the
morning, a rhythmic, quick-cadenced walking
around the dining-room table. My mother was
asleep in one room upstairs, my brother Herman in
another; grandfather was in the attic, in the old
walnut bed which, as you will remember, once fell
on my father. I had just stepped out of the bathtub
and was busily rubbing myself with a towel when I
heard the steps. They were the steps of a man walking rapidly around the dining-room table downstairs. The light from the bathroom shone down the

back steps, which dropped directly into the dining-room; I could see the faint shine of plates on the plate-rail; I couldn't see the table. The steps kept going round and round the table; at regular intervals a board creaked, when it was trod upon. I supposed at first that it was my father or my brother Roy, who had gone to Indianapolis but were expected home at any time. I suspected next that it was a burglar. It did not enter my mind until later that it was a ghost.

After the walking had gone on for perhaps three minutes, I tiptoed to Herman's room. 'Psst!' I hissed, in the dark, shaking him. 'Awp,' he said, in the low, hopeless tone of a despondent beagle – he always half suspected that something would 'get him' in the night. I told him who I was. 'There's something downstairs!' I said. He got up and followed me to the head of the back staircase. We listened together. There was no sound. The steps had ceased. Herman looked at me in some alarm: I had only the bath towel around my waist. He wanted to go back to bed, but I gripped his arm. 'There's something down there!' I said. Instantly the steps began again, circled the dining-room table like a man running, and started up the stairs toward us, heavily, two at a time. The light still shone palely down the stairs; we saw nothing coming; we only heard the steps. Herman rushed to his room and slammed the door. I slammed shut the door at the stairs top and held my knee against it. After a long minute, I slowly opened it again. There was nothing there. There was no sound. None of us ever heard the ghost again.

The slamming of the doors had aroused mother: she peered out of her room. 'What on earth are you boys doing?' she demanded. Herman ventured out of his room. 'Nothing,' he said, gruffly, but he was, in colour, a light green. 'What was all that running around downstairs?' said mother. So she had heard the steps, too! We just looked at her. 'Burglars!' she shouted intuitively. I tried to quiet her by starting lightly downstairs.

'Come on, Herman,' I said.

'I'll stay with mother,' he said. 'She's all excited.'

I stepped back on to the landing.

'Don't either of you go a step,' said mother. 'We'll call the police.' Since the phone was downstairs, I didn't see how we were going to call the police – nor did I want the police – but mother made one of her quick, incomparable decisions. She flung up a window of her bedroom, which faced the bedroom windows of the house of a neighbour, picked up a shoe, and whammed it through a pane of glass across the narrow space that separated the two houses. Glass tinkled into the bedroom occupied by a retired engraver named Bodwell and his wife. Bodwell had been for some years in rather a bad way and was subject to mild 'attacks'. Most everybody we knew or lived near had *some* kind of attacks.

It was now about two o'clock of a moonless night; clouds hung black and low. Bodwell was at the window in a minute, shouting, frothing a little, shaking his fist. 'We'll sell the house and go back to Peoria,' we could hear Mrs Bodwell saying. It was some time before mother 'got through' to Bodwell. 'Burglars!' she shouted. 'Burglars in the house!' Herman and I hadn't dared to tell her that it was not burglars but ghosts, for she was even more afraid of ghosts than of burglars. Bodwell at first thought that she meant there were burglars in his house, but finally he quieted down and called the police for us over an extension phone by his bed. After he had disappeared from the window, mother suddenly made as if to throw another shoe, not because there was further need of it but, as she later explained, because the thrill of heaving a shoe through a window glass had enormously taken her fancy. I prevented her.

The police were on hand in a commendably short time: a Ford sedan full of them, two on motorcycles, and a patrol wagon with about eight in it and a few reporters. They began banging at our front door. Flashlights shot streaks of gleam up and down the walls, across the yard, down the walk between our house and Bodwell's. 'Open up!' cried a hoarse voice. 'We're men from Headquarters!' I wanted to go down and let them in, since there they were, but mother wouldn't hear of it. 'You haven't a stitch on,' she pointed out. 'You'd catch your death.' I wound the towel around me again. Finally the cops put their shoulders to our big heavy front door with its thick bevelled glass and broke it in: I could hear a rending of wood and a splash of glass on the floor of the hall. Their lights played all over the living-room and criss-crossed nervously in the dining-room, stabbed into hallways, shot up the front stairs and finally up the back. They caught me standing in my towel at the top. A heavy policeman bounded up the steps. 'Who are you?' he demanded. 'I live here,' I said. 'Well whattsa matta, ya hot?' he asked. It was, as a matter of fact, cold; I went to my room and pulled on some trousers. On my way out, a cop stuck a gun into my ribs. 'Whatta you doin' here?' he demanded.

'I live here,' I said.

The officer in charge reported to mother. 'No sign of nobody, lady,' he said. 'Musta got away – whatt'd he look like?' 'There were two or three of them,' mother said, 'whooping and carrying on and slamming doors.' 'Funny,' said the cop. 'All ya windows and doors was locked on the inside tight as a tick.'

Downstairs, we could hear the tromping of the other police. Police were all over the place; doors were yanked open, drawers were yanked open, windows were shot up and pulled down, furniture fell with dull thumps. A half-dozen policemen emerged out of the darkness of the front hallway upstairs. They began to ransack the floor: pulled beds away from walls, tore clothes off hooks in the closets, pulled suitcases and boxes off shelves. One of them found an old zither that Roy had won in a pool tournament. 'Looky here, Joe,' he said strumming it with a big paw. The cop named Joe took it and turned it over. 'What is it?' he asked me. 'It's an old zither our guinea pig used to sleep on,' I said. It was true that a pet guinea pig we once had would never sleep anywhere except on the zither, but I should never have said so. Joe and the other cop looked at me a long time. They put the zither back on a shelf.

'No sign o' nuthin',' said the cop who had first spoken to mother. 'This guy,' he explained to the others, jerking a thumb at me, 'was nekked. The lady seems historical.' They all nodded, but said nothing; just looked at me. In the small silence we all heard a creaking in the attic. Grandfather was turning over in bed. 'What's 'at?' snapped Joe. Five or six cops sprang for the attic door before I could intervene or explain. I realised that it would be bad if they burst in on grandfather unannounced or even announced. He was going through a phase in which he believed that General Meade's men, under steady hammering by Stonewall Jackson, were beginning to retreat and even desert.

When I got to the attic, things were pretty

confused. Grandfather had evidently jumped to the conclusion that the police were deserters from Meade's army, trying to hide away in his attic. He bounded out of bed wearing a long flannel nightgown over long woollen underwear, a nightcap, and a leather jacket around his chest. The cops must have realised at once that the indignant white-haired old man belonged in the house, but they had no chance to say so. 'Back, ye cowardly dogs!' roared grandfather. 'Back t' the lines, ye goddam lily-livered cattle!' With that, he fetched the officer who found the zither a flat-handed smack alongside his head that sent him sprawling. The others beat a retreat, but not fast enough; grandfather grabbed Zither's gun from its holster and let fly. The report seemed to crack the rafters; smoke filled the attic. A cop cursed and shot his hand to his shoulder. Somehow, we all finally got downstairs again and locked the door against the old gentleman. He fired once or twice more in the darkness and then went back to bed. 'That was grandfather,' I explained to Joe, out of breath. 'He thinks you're deserters.' 'I'll say he does,' said Joe.

The cops were reluctant to leave without getting their hands on somebody besides grandfather; the night had been distinctly a defeat for them. Furthermore, they obviously didn't like the 'layout', something looked – and I can see their viewpoint – phony. They began to poke into things again. A reporter, a thin-faced, wispy man, came up to me. I had put on one of mother's blouses, not being able to find anything else. The reporter looked at me with mingled suspicion and interest. 'Just what the hell is the real lowdown here, Bud?' he asked. I decided to be frank with him. 'We had ghosts,' I said. He gazed at me a long time as if I were a slot machine into which he had, without results, dropped a nickel. Then he walked away. The cops followed him, the one grandfather shot holding his now-bandaged arm, cursing and blaspheming. 'I'm gonna get my gun back from that old bird,' said the zither-cop. 'Yeh,' said Joe. 'You – and who else?' I told them I would bring it to the station house the next day.

'What was the matter with that one policeman?' mother asked, after they had gone. 'Grandfather shot him,' I said. 'What for?' she demanded. I told her he was a deserter. 'Of all things!' said mother. 'He was such a nice-looking young man.'

Grandfather was fresh as a daisy and full of jokes at breakfast next morning. We thought at first he had forgotten all about what had happened, but he hadn't. Over his third cup of coffee, he glared at Herman and me. 'What was the idee of all them cops tarryhootin' round the house last night?' he demanded. He had us there.

Sonata For Harp and Bicycle

Joan Aiken

'No one is allowed to remain in the building after five p.m.,' Mr Manaby told his new assistant, showing him into the little room that was like the inside of an egg carton.

'Why not?'

'Directorial policy,' said Mr Manaby. But that was not the real reason.

Gaunt and sooty, Grimes Buildings lurched up the side of a hill towards Clerkenwell. Every little office within its dim and crumbling exterior owned one tiny crumb of light – such was the proud boast of the architect – but towards evening the crumbs were collected, absorbed and demolished as by an immense vacuum cleaner, and yielded to an uncontrollable mass of dark that came tumbling in through windows and doors to take their place. Darkness infested the building like a flight of bats returning willingly to roost.

'Wash hands, please. Wash hands, please,' the intercom began to bawl in the passages at four-forty-five. Without much need of prompting the staff hustled like lemmings along the corridors to the green and blue-tiled washrooms that mocked the encroaching dusk with an illusion of cheerfulness.

'All papers into cases, please,' the Tannoy warned, five minutes later. 'Look at your desks, ladies and gentlemen. Any documents left lying about? Kindly put them away. Desks must be left clear and tidy. Drawers must be shut.'

A multitudinous shuffling, a rustling as of innumerable bluebottles might have been heard by the attentive ear after this injunction, as the employees of Moreton Wold and Company thrust their papers into briefcases, hurried letters and invoices into drawers, clipped statistical abstracts together and slammed them into filing cabinets; dropped discarded copy into wastepaper baskets. Two minutes later, and not a desk throughout Grimes Buildings bore more than its customary coating of dust.

'Hats and coats on, please. Hats and coats on, please. Did you bring an umbrella? Have you left any shopping on the floor?'

At three minutes to five the home-going throng was in the lifts and on the stairs; a clattering staccato-voiced flood momentarily darkened the great double doors of the building, and then as the first faint notes of St Paul's came echoing faintly on the frosty air, to be picked up near at hand by the louder chime of St Biddulph's on the Wall, the entire premises of Moreton Wold stood empty.

'But why is it?' Jason Ashgrove, the new copy-writer, asked his secretary. 'Why are the staff herded out so fast in the evenings? Not that I'm against it, mind you, I think it's an admirable idea in many ways, but there is the liberty of the individual to be considered, don't you think?'

'Hush!' Miss Golden, casting a glance towards the

door, held up her felt-tip in warning or reproof. 'You mustn't ask that sort of question. When you are taken on to the Established Staff you'll be told. Not before.'

'But I want to know now,' said Jason in discontent. 'Do you know?'

'Yes I do,' Miss Golden answered tantalisingly. 'Come on, or we shan't have done the Oat Crisp layout by a quarter to.' And she stared firmly down at the copy in front of her, lips folded, candyfloss hair falling over her face, lashes hiding eyes like peridots, a girl with a secret.

Jason was annoyed. He rapped out a couple of rude and witty rhymes which Miss Golden let pass in a withering silence.

'What do you want for Christmas, Miss Golden? Sherry? Fudge? Bath cubes?'

'I want to go away with a clear conscience about Oat Crisps,' Miss Golden retorted. It was not true; what she chiefly wanted was Mr Jason Ashgrove, but he had not realised this yet.

'Come on, don't be a tease! I'm sure you haven't been on the Established Staff all that long,' he coaxed her. 'What happens when one is taken on, anyway? Does the Managing Director have us up for a confidential chat? Or are we given a little book called The Awful Secret of Grimes Buildings?'

Miss Golden wasn't telling. She opened her desk drawer and took out a white towel and a cake of rosy soap.

'Wash hands, please! Wash hands, please!'

Jason was frustrated. 'You'll be sorry,' he said. 'I shall do something desperate.'

'Oh no, you mustn't!' Her eyes were large with fright. She ran from the room and was back within a couple of minutes, still drying her hands.

'If I took you out to dinner, wouldn't you give me just a tiny hint?'

Side by side Miss Golden and Mr Ashgrove ran along the green-floored corridors, battled down the white marble stairs, among the hundred other employees from the tenth floor, and the nine hundred from the floors below.

He saw her lips move as she said something, but in the clatter of two thousand feet the words were lost.

'. . . f-f-fire-escape,' he heard, as they came into the momentary hush of the coir-carpeted entrance hall. And '. . . it's to do with a bicycle. A bicycle and a harp.'

'I don't understand.'

Now they were in the street, chilly with the winter-dusk smells of celery on barrows, of swept-up leaves heaped in faraway parks, and cold layers of dew sinking among the withered evening primroses in the building sites. London lay about them wreathed in twilit mystery and fading against the barred and smoky sky. Like a ninth wave the sound of traffic overtook and swallowed them.

'Please tell me!'

But, shaking her head, she stepped on to a scarlet home-bound bus and was borne away from him.

Jason stood undecided on the pavement, with the crowds dividing round him as round the pier of a bridge. He scratched his head and looked about him for guidance.

An ambulance clanged, a taxi screeched, a drill stuttered, a siren wailed on the river, a door slammed, a van hooted, and close beside his ear a bicycle bell tinkled its tiny warning.

A bicycle, she had said. A bicycle and a harp.

Jason turned and stared at Grimes Buildings. Somewhere, he knew, there was a back way in, a service entrance. He walked slowly past the main doors, with their tubs of snowy chrysanthemums, and on up Glass Street. A tiny furtive wedge of darkness beckoned him, a snicket, a hacket, an alley carved into the thickness of the building. It was so narrow that at any moment, it seemed, the over-topping walls would come together and squeeze it out of existence.

Walking as softly as an Indian, Jason passed through it, slid by a file of dustbins, and found the foot of the fire-escape. Iron treads rose into the mist, like an illustration to a Gothic fairytale.

He began to climb.

When he had mounted to the ninth storey he paused for breath. It was a lonely place. The lighting consisted of a dim bulb at the foot of every flight. A well of gloom sank beneath him. The cold fingers of the wind nagged and fluttered at the edges of his jacket, and he pulled the string of the fire-door and edged inside.

Grimes Buildings were triangular, with the street forming the base of the triangle, and the fire-escape the point. Jason could see two long passages coming towards him, meeting at an acute angle where he stood. He started down the left-hand one, tiptoeing in the cave-like silence. Nowhere was there any sound, except for the faraway drip of a tap. No nightwatchman would stay in the building; none was needed. No precautions were taken. Burglars gave the place a wide berth.

Jason opened a door at random; then another. Offices lay everywhere about him, empty and for-bidding. Some held lipstick-stained tissues, spilt powder, and orange-peel; others were still foggy with cigarette smoke. Here was a director's suite of rooms – a desk like half an acre of frozen lake, inch-thick carpet, roses, and the smell of cigars. Here was a conference room with scattered squares of doodled blotting-paper. All equally empty.

He was not sure when he first began to notice the bell. Telephone, he thought at first, and then he remembered that all the outside lines were disconnected at five. And this bell, anyway, had not the regularity of a telephone's double ring: there was a tinkle, and then silence: a long ring, and then silence: a whole volley of rings together, and then silence.

Jason stood listening, and fear knocked against his ribs and shortened his breath. He knew that he must move or be paralysed by it. He ran up a flight of stairs and found himself with two more endless green corridors beckoning him like a pair of dividers.

Another sound now: a waft of ice-thin notes, riffling up an arpeggio like a flurry of sleet. Far away down the passage it echoed. Jason ran in pursuit, but as he ran the music receded. He circled the building, but it always outdistanced him, and when he came back to the stairs he heard it fading away on to the storey below.

He hesitated, and as he did so, heard once more the bell: the bicycle bell. It was approaching him fast, bearing down on him, urgent, menacing. He could hear the pedals, almost see the shimmer of an invisible wheel. Absurdly, he was reminded of the insistent clamour of an ice-cream vendor, summoning children on a sultry Sunday afternoon.

There was a little fireman's alcove beside him, with buckets and pumps. He hurled himself into it. The bell stopped beside him, and then there was a moment while his heart tried to shake itself loose in his chest. He was looking into two eyes carved out of expressionless air; he was held by two hands knotted together out of the width of dark.

'Daisy? Daisy?' came the whisper. 'Is that you, Daisy? Have you come to give me your answer?'

Jason tried to speak, but no words came.

'It's *not* Daisy! Who are you?' The sibilants were full of threat. 'You can't stay here! This is private property.'

He was thrust along the corridor. It was like being pushed by a whirlwind – the fire door opened ahead of him without a touch, and he was on the openwork platform, clutching the slender railing. Still the hands would not let him go.

'How about it?' the whisper mocked him. 'How about jumping? It's an easy death compared with some.'

Jason looked down into the smoky void. The darkness nodded to him like a familiar.

'You wouldn't be much loss, would you? What have you got to live for?'

Miss Golden, Jason thought. She would miss me. And the syllables Berenice Golden lingered in the air like a chime. Drawing on some unknown deposit of courage he shook himself loose from the holding hands, and ran down the fire escape without looking back.

Next morning when Miss Golden, crisp, fragrant and punctual, shut the door of Room 92 behind her, she stopped short by the hat-pegs with a horrified gasp.

'Mr *Ashgrove!* Your *hair!*'

'It makes me look very distinguished, don't you think?' he said.

It did indeed have this effect, for his Byronic dark cut had changed to a stippled silver.

'How did it happen? You've not –' her voice sank to a whisper – '*You've not been in Grimes Buildings after dark?*'

'What if I have?'

'Have you?'

'Miss Golden – Berenice,' he said earnestly. 'Who was Daisy? I can see that you know. Tell me her story.'

'Did you see him?' she asked faintly.

'Him?'

'William Heron – the Wailing Watchman. Oh,' she exclaimed in terror. 'I can see that you must have. Then you are doomed – doomed!'

'If I'm doomed,' said Jason, 'let's have coffee and you tell me all about it.'

'It all happened over fifty years ago,' said Berenice, as she spooned out coffee powder with distracted extravagance. 'Heron was the night-watchman in this building, patrolling the corridors from dusk to dawn every night on his bicycle. He fell in love with a Miss Bell who taught the harp. She rented a room – this room – and gave lessons in it. She began to reciprocate his love, and they used to share a picnic supper every night at eleven, and she'd stay on a while to keep him company. It was an idyll, among the fire-buckets and the furnace-pipes.

'On Christmas Eve he had summoned up the courage to propose to her. The day before he had told her that he was going to ask her a very impor-tant question. Next night he came to the Buildings with a huge bunch of roses and a bottle of wine. But Miss Bell never turned up.

'The explanation was simple. Miss Bell, of course, had been losing a lot of sleep through her nocturnal romance, as she gave lessons all day, and so she used to take a nap in her music-room between seven and ten every evening, to save going home. In order to make sure that she would wake up, she persuaded her father, a distant relation of Graham Bell who shared some of the more famous Bell's mechanical ingenuity, to install an alarm device, a kind of telephone, in her room, which called her every evening at ten. She was far too modest and shy to let Heron know that she spent those hours actually in the building, and to give him the chance of waking her himself.

'Alas! On this important evening the gadget failed and she never woke up. Telephones were in their infancy at that time, you must remember.

'Heron waited and waited. At last, mad with grief and jealousy, having rung up her home and discovered that she was not there, he concluded that she had rejected him, ran to the fire-escape, and cast himself off it, holding the roses and the bottle of wine. He jumped from the tenth floor.

'Daisy did not long survive him, but pined away soon after; since that day their ghosts have haunted Grimes Buildings, he vainly patrolling the corridors on his bicycle in search of her, she playing her harp in the small room she rented. *But they never meet.* And anyone who meets the ghost of William Heron will himself within five days leap down from the same fatal fire-escape.'

She gazed at him with tragic eyes.

'In that case we mustn't lose a minute,' said Jason and he enveloped her in an embrace as prolonged as it was ardent. Looking down at the gossamer hair sprayed across his shoulder, he added, 'Just the same, it is a preposterous situation. Firstly, I have no intention of jumping off the fire-escape — ' here, however, he repressed a shudder as he remembered the cold, clutching hands of the evening before –

'And secondly, I find it quite nonsensical that those two inefficient ghosts have spent fifty years in this building without coming across each other. We must remedy the matter, Berenice. We must not begrudge our new-found happiness to others.'

He gave her another kiss so impassioned that the electric typewriter against which they were leaning began chattering to itself in a frenzy of enthusiasm.

'This very evening,' he went on, looking at his watch, 'we will put matters right for that unhappy couple, and then, if I really have only five more days to live, which I don't for one moment believe, we will proceed to spend them together, my bewitching Berenice, in the most advantageous manner possible.'

She nodded, spellbound.

'Can you work a switchboard?' She nodded again. 'My love, you are perfection itself. Meet me in the switchboard room, then, at ten this evening. I would say, have dinner with me, but I shall need to make one or two purchases and see an old R.A.F. friend. You will be safe from Heron's curse in the switchboard room if he always keeps to the corridors.'

'I would rather meet him and die with you,' she murmured.

'My angel, I hope that won't be necessary. Now,' he said sighing, 'I suppose we should get down to our day's work.' Strangely enough, the copy they wrote that day, although engendered from such agitated minds, sold more packets of Oat Crisps than any other advertising matter before or since.

That evening when Jason entered Grimes Buildings he was carrying two bottles of wine, two bunches of red roses, and a large canvas-covered bundle. Miss

Golden, who had concealed herself in the telephone exchange before the offices closed for the night, gazed at these things with interest.

'Now,' said Jason after he had greeted her, 'I want you first of all to ring our own extension.'

'No one will reply, surely?'

'I think *she* will reply.'

Sure enough, when Berenice rang extension 170 a faint, sleepy voice, distant and yet clear, whispered, 'Hullo?'

'Is that Miss Bell?'

'. . . Yes.'

Berenice went a little pale. Her eyes sought Jason's and, prompted by him, she said formally, 'Switchboard here, Miss Bell, your ten o' clock call.'

'Thank you,' whispered the telephone.

'Excellent,' Jason remarked, as Miss Golden replaced the receiver with a trembling hand. He unfastened his package and slipped its straps over his shoulders. 'Now, plug in the intercom.'

Berenice did so, and then announced, loudly and clearly, 'Attention. Night watchman on duty, please. Night watchman on duty. You have an urgent summons to Room 92. You have an urgent summons to Room 92.'

Her voice echoed and reverberated through the empty corridors, then the Tannoy coughed itself to silence.

'Now we must run. You take the roses, sweetheart, and I'll carry the bottles.'

Together they raced up eight flights of stairs and along the green corridor to Room 92. As they neared the door a burst of music met them – harp music swelling out, sweet and triumphant. Jason took one of the bunches of roses from Berenice, opened the door a little way, and gently deposited the flowers, with the bottle, inside the door. As he closed it again Berenice said breathlessly, 'Did you see anything?'

'No,' he said. 'The room was too full of music.' His eyes were shining.

They stood hand in hand, reluctant to move away, waiting for they hardly knew what. Suddenly the door flew open again. Neither Berenice nor Jason, afterwards, cared to speak of what they saw then, but each was left with a memory, bright as the picture on a Salvador Dali calendar, of a bicycle bearing on its saddle a harp, a bottle of wine, and a bouquet of red roses, sweeping improbably down the corridor and far, far away.

'We can go now,' said Jason. He led Berenice to the fire door, tucking the other bottle of Mâcon into his jacket pocket. A black wind from the north whistled beneath, as they stood on the openwork iron platform, looking down.

'We don't want our evening to be spoilt by the thought of that curse hanging over us,' he said, 'so this is the practical thing to do. Hang on to the roses.' And holding his love firmly, Jason pulled the ripcord of his R.A.F. friend's parachute and leapt off the fire-escape.

A bridal shower of rose petals adorned the descent of Miss Golden, who was possibly the only girl to be kissed in mid-air in the district of Clerkenwell at ten minutes to midnight on Christmas Eve.

Jimmy Takes Vanishing Lessons

Walter R. Brooks

The school bus picked up Jimmy Crandall every morning at the side road that led up to his aunt's house, and every afternoon it dropped him there again. And so twice a day, on the bus, he passed the entrance to the mysterious road.

It wasn't much of a road any more. It was choked with weeds and blackberry bushes, and the woods on both sides pressed in so closely that the branches met overhead, and it was dark and gloomy even on bright days. The bus driver once pointed it out.

'Folks that go in there after dark,' he said, 'well, they usually don't ever come out again. There's a haunted house about a quarter of a mile down that road.' He paused. 'But you ought to know about that, Jimmy. It was your grandfather's house.'

Jimmy knew about it, and he knew that it now belonged to his Aunt Mary. But Jimmy's aunt would never talk to him about the house. She said the stories about it were silly nonsense and there were no such things as ghosts. If all the villagers weren't a lot of superstitious idiots, she would be

26

able to let the house, and then she would have enough money to buy Jimmy some decent clothes and take him to the cinema.

Jimmy thought it was all very well to say that there were no such things as ghosts but how about the people who had tried to live there? Aunt Mary had let the house three times, but every family had moved out within a week. They said the things that went on there were just too queer. So nobody would live in it any more.

Jimmy thought about the house a lot. If he could only prove that there wasn't a ghost . . . And one Saturday when his aunt was in the village, Jimmy took the key to the haunted house from its hook on the kitchen door, and started out.

It had seemed like a fine idea when he had first thought of it – to find out for himself. Even in the silence and damp gloom of the old road it still seemed pretty good. Nothing to be scared of, he told himself. Ghosts aren't around in the daytime. But when he came out in the clearing and looked at those blank, dusty windows, he wasn't so sure.

'Oh, come on!' he told himself. And he squared his shoulders and waded through the long grass to the porch.

Then he stopped again. His feet did not seem to want to go up the steps. It took him nearly five minutes to persuade them to move. But when at last they did, they marched right up and across the porch to the front door, and Jimmy set his teeth hard and put the key in the keyhole. It turned with a squeak. He pushed the door open and went in.

That was probably the bravest thing that Jimmy had ever done. He was in a long dark hall with closed doors on both sides, and on the right there were stairs going up. He had left the door open behind him, and the light from it showed him that, except for the hat-rack and table and chairs, the hall was empty. And then as he stood there, listening to the bumping of his heart, gradually the light faded, the hall grew darker and darker – as if something huge had come up on the porch behind him and stood there, blocking the doorway. He swung round quickly, but there was nothing there.

He drew a deep breath. It must have been just a cloud passing across the sun. But then the door, all by itself, began to swing shut. And before he could stop it, it closed with a bang. And it was then, as he was pulling frantically at the handle to get out, that Jimmy saw the ghost.

It behaved just as you would expect a ghost to behave. It was a tall, dim, white figure, and it came gliding slowly down the stairs towards him. Jimmy gave a yell, yanked the door open, and tore down the steps.

He didn't stop until he was well down the road. Then he had to get his breath. He sat down on a log. 'Boy!' he said. 'I've seen a ghost! Golly, was that awful!' Then after a minute he thought, 'What was so awful about it? He was trying to scare me, like that smart aleck who was always jumping out from behind things. Pretty silly business for a grown-up ghost to be doing.'

It always makes you cross when someone deliberately tries to scare you. And as Jimmy got over his fright, he began to get angry. And pretty soon he got up and stared back. 'I must get that key, anyway,' he thought, for he had left it in the door.

This time he approached very quietly. He thought he'd just lock the door and go home. But as he tiptoed up the steps he saw it was still open; and as he reached out cautiously for the key, he heard a faint sound. He drew back and peeped round the door-jamb, and there was the ghost.

The ghost was going back upstairs, but he wasn't gliding now, he was doing a sort of dance, and every other step he would bend double and shake with laughter. His thin cackle was the sound Jimmy had heard. Evidently he was enjoying the joke he had played.

That made Jimmy crosser than ever. He stuck his head farther around the door-jamb and yelled 'Boo!' at the top of his lungs. The ghost gave a thin shriek and leaped two feet in the air, then collapsed on the stairs.

As soon as Jimmy saw he could scare the ghost even worse than the ghost could scare him, he wasn't afraid any more and he came right into the hall. The ghost was hanging on the banister and panting. 'Oh my goodness!' he gasped. 'Oh, my gracious! Boy, you can't do that to me!'

'I did it, didn't I?' said Jimmy. 'Now we're even.'

'Nothing of the kind,' said the ghost crossly. 'You seem pretty stupid, even for a boy. Ghosts are supposed to scare people. People aren't supposed to scare ghosts.' He got up slowly and glided down and sat on the bottom step. 'But look here, boy; this could be pretty serious for me if people got to know about it.'

'You mean you don't want me to tell anybody about it?' Jimmy asked.

'Suppose we make a deal,' the ghost said. 'You keep quiet about this, and in return I'll – well, let's see; how would you like to know how to vanish?'

'Oh, that would be swell!' Jimmy exclaimed. 'But – can you vanish?'

'Sure,' said the ghost, and he did. All at once he just wasn't there. Jimmy was alone in the hall.

But his voice went right on. 'It would be pretty handy, wouldn't it?' he said persuasively. 'You could get into the cinema free whenever you wanted to, and if your aunt called you to do something – when you were in the garden, say – well, she wouldn't be able to find you.'

'I don't mind helping Aunt Mary,' Jimmy said.

'H'm. High-minded, eh?' said the ghost. 'Well, then . . .'

'I wish you'd please reappear,' Jimmy interrupted. 'It makes me feel funny to talk to somebody who isn't there.'

'Sorry, I forgot,' said the ghost, and there he was again, sitting on the bottom step. Jimmy could see the step, dimly, right through him. 'Good trick, eh? Well, if you don't like vanishing, maybe I could teach you to seep through keyholes. Like this.' He floated over to the door and went right through the keyhole, the way water goes down the drain. Then he came back the same way.

'That's useful, too,' he said. 'Getting into locked rooms and so on. You can go anywhere the wind can.'

'No,' said Jimmy. 'There's only one thing you can do to get me to promise not to tell about scaring you. Go and live somewhere else. There's Miller's up the road. Nobody lives there any more.'

'That old shack!' said the ghost, with a nasty laugh. 'Doors and windows half off, roof leaky – no thanks! What do you think it's like in a storm, windows banging, rain dripping on you – I guess not! Peace and quiet, that's really what a ghost wants out of life.'

'Well, I don't think it's very fair,' Jimmy said, 'for you to live in a house that doesn't belong to you and keep my aunt from letting it.'

'Pooh!' said the ghost. 'I'm not stopping her from letting it. I don't take up any room, and it's not my fault if people get scared and leave.'

'It certainly is!' Jimmy said angrily. 'You don't play fair and I'm not going to make any bargain with you. I'm going to tell everybody how I scared you.'

'Oh, you mustn't do that!' The ghost seemed quite disturbed and he vanished and reappeared rapidly several times. 'If that got out, every ghost in the country would be in terrible trouble.'

So they argued about it. The ghost said if Jimmy wanted money he could learn to vanish; then he could join a circus and get a big salary. Jimmy said he didn't want to be in a circus; he wanted to go to college and learn to be a doctor. He was very firm. And the ghost began to cry. 'But this is my home, boy,' he said. 'Thirty years I've lived here and no trouble to anybody, and now you want to throw me out into the cold world! And for what? A little money! That's pretty heartless.' And he sobbed, trying to make Jimmy feel cruel.

Jimmy didn't feel cruel at all, for the ghost had certainly driven plenty of other people out into the cold world. But he didn't really think it would do much good for him to tell anybody that he had scared the ghost. Nobody would believe him, and how could he prove it? So after a minute he said, 'Well, all right. You teach me to vanish and I won't tell.' They settled it that way.

Jimmy didn't say anything to his aunt about what he'd done. But every Saturday he went to the haunted house for his vanishing lesson. It is really quite easy when you know how, and in a couple of weeks he could flicker, and in six weeks the ghost gave him an examination and he got a B plus, which is very good for a human. So he thanked the ghost and shook hands with him and said, 'Well, goodbye now. You'll hear from me.'

'What do you mean by that?' said the ghost suspiciously. But Jimmy just laughed and ran off home.

That night at supper Jimmy's aunt said, 'Well what have you been doing today?'

'I've been learning to vanish.'

His aunt smiled and said, 'That must be fun.'

'Honestly,' said Jimmy. 'The ghost up at Grandfather's house taught me.'

'I don't think that's very funny,' said his aunt. 'And will you please not – why, where are you?' she demanded, for he had vanished.

'Here, Aunt Mary,' he said as he reappeared.

'Merciful heavens!' she exclaimed, and she pushed back her chair and rubbed her eyes hard. Then she looked at him again.

Well, it took a lot of explaining and he had to do it twice more before he could persuade her that he really could vanish. She was pretty upset. But at last she calmed down and they had a long talk. Jimmy kept his word and didn't tell her that he had scared the ghost, but he said he had a plan and at last, though very reluctantly, she agreed to help him.

So the next day she went up to the old house and started to work. She opened the windows and swept and dusted and aired the bedding and made as much noise as possible. This disturbed the ghost, and pretty soon he came floating into the room where she was sweeping. She was scared all right. She gave a yell and threw the broom at him. As the broom went right through him and he came nearer, waving his arms and groaning, she shrank back.

And Jimmy, who had been standing there invisible all the time, suddenly appeared and jumped at the ghost with a 'Boo!' and the ghost fell over in a dead faint.

As soon as Jimmy's aunt saw that, she wasn't frightened any more. She found some smelling salts and held them under the ghost's nose, and when he came to she tried to help him into a chair. Of course, she couldn't help him. But at last he sat up and said reproachfully to Jimmy, 'You broke your word!'

'I promised not to tell about scaring you!' said the boy, 'but I didn't promise not to scare you again.'

And his aunt said, 'You really are a ghost, aren't you? I thought you were just stories people made up. Well, excuse me, but I must get on with my work.' And she began sweeping and banging around with her broom harder than ever.

The ghost put his hands to his head. 'All this noise,' he said. 'Couldn't you work more quietly, ma'am?'

'Whose house is this anyway?' she demanded. 'If you don't like it, why don't you move out?'

The ghost sneezed violently several times. 'Excuse me,' he said. 'You're raising so much dust. Where's that boy?' he asked suddenly. For Jimmy had vanished again.

'I'm sure I don't know,' she replied. 'Probably getting ready to scare you again.'

'You ought to have better control of him,' said the ghost severely. 'If he was my boy, I'd take a hairbrush to him.'

'You have my permission,' she said, and she reached right through the ghost and pulled the chair cushion out from under him and began banging the dust out of it. 'What's more,' she went on, as he got up and glided wearily to another chair. 'Jimmy and I are going to sleep here at night from now on, and I don't think it would be very clever of you to try any tricks.'

'Ha, ha,' said the ghost nastily. 'He who laughs last . . . .'

'Ha, ha, yourself,' said Jimmy's voice from close behind him. 'And that's me, laughing last.'

The ghost muttered and vanished.

Jimmy's aunt put cottonwool in her ears and slept that night in the best bedroom with the light lit. The ghost screamed for a while down in the cellar, but nothing happened, so he came upstairs. He thought he would appear to her as two glaring, fiery eyes, which was one of his best tricks, but first he wanted to be sure where Jimmy was. But he couldn't find him. He hunted all over the house and, though he was invisible himself, he got more and more nervous. He kept imagining that at any moment Jimmy might jump out at him from some dark corner and scare him into fits. Finally he got so jittery that he went back to the cellar and hid in the coal bin all night.

The following days were just as bad for the ghost. Several times he tried to scare Jimmy's aunt while she was working, but she didn't take any notice, and twice Jimmy managed to sneak up on him and appear suddenly with a loud yell, frightening him dreadfully. He was, I suppose, rather timid even for a ghost. He began to look quite haggard. He had several long arguments with Jimmy's aunt, in which he wept and appealed to her sympathy, but she was firm. If he wanted to live there he would have to pay rent, just like anybody else. There was the abandoned Miller farm two miles up the road. Why didn't he move there?

When the house was all in apple-pie order, Jimmy's aunt went down to the village to see a Mr and Mrs Whistler, who were living at the hotel because they couldn't find a house to move into. She told them about the old house, but they said, 'No, thank you. We've heard about that house. It's haunted. I'll bet,' they said, 'you wouldn't dare spend a night there.'

She told them that she had spent the last week there, but they evidently didn't believe her. So she said, 'You know my nephew, Jimmy. He's twelve years old. I am so sure that the house is not haunted that, if you want to rent it, I will let Jimmy stay there with you every night until you are sure everything is all right.'

'Ha!' said Mr Whistler. 'The boy won't do it. He's got more sense.'

So they sent for Jimmy. 'Why, I've spent the last week there,' he said. 'Of course I will.'

But the Whistlers still refused.

So Jimmy's aunt went round and told a lot of the village people about their talk, and everybody made so much fun of the Whistlers for being afraid, when a twelve-year-old boy wasn't, that they were ashamed, and said they would rent it. So they moved in.

Jimmy stayed there for a week, but he saw nothing of the ghost. And then one day one of the boys in his class told him that somebody had seen a ghost up at the Miller farm. So Jimmy knew the ghost had taken his aunt's advice.

A day or two later he walked up to the Miller's farm. There was no front door and he walked right in. There was some groaning and thumping upstairs, and then after a minute the ghost came floating down.

'Oh, it's you!' he said. 'Goodness' sakes, boy, can't you leave me in peace?'

Jimmy said he'd just come up to see how he was getting along.

'Getting along fine,' said the ghost. 'From my point of view it's a very desirable property. Peaceful. Quiet. Nobody playing silly tricks.'

'Well,' said Jimmy, 'I won't bother you if you don't bother the Whistlers. But if you come back there . . . .'

'Don't worry,' said the ghost.

So with the rent money, Jimmy and his aunt had a much easier life. They went to the cinema sometimes twice a week, and Jimmy had all new clothes, and on Thanksgiving, for the first time in his life, Jimmy had a turkey.

Once a week he would go up the Miller farm to see the ghost and they got to be very good friends. The ghost even came down to the Thanksgiving dinner, though of course he couldn't eat much. He seemed to enjoy the warmth of the house and he was in very good humour. He taught Jimmy several more tricks. The best one was how to glare with fiery eyes, which was useful later on when Jimmy became a doctor and had to look down people's throats to see if their tonsils ought to come out. He was really a pretty good fellow as ghosts go, and Jimmy's aunt got quite fond of him herself.

When the real winter weather began, she even used to worry about him a lot, because, of course, there was no heat in the Miller place and the doors and windows didn't amount to much and there was hardly any roof. The ghost tried to explain to her that the heat and cold didn't bother ghosts at all.

'Maybe not,' she said, 'but just the same, it can't be very pleasant.' And when he accepted their invitation for Christmas dinner she knitted some red woollen slippers, and he was so pleased that he broke down and cried. And that made Jimmy's aunt so happy, she broke down and cried.

Jimmy didn't cry, but he said, 'Aunt Mary, don't you think it would be nice if the ghost came down and lived with us this winter?'

'I would feel very much better about him if he did,' she said.

So he stayed with them that winter, and then he just stayed on, and it must have been a peaceful place for the last I heard he was still there.

The Murderous Ghosts

Rosemary Timperley

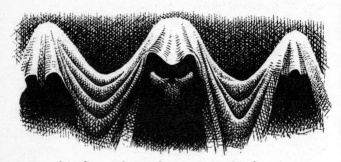

It was his first Channel crossing. His first journey abroad, in fact. Abroad. Another world. And the sea had to be crossed before one got there. It was exciting. Strange, too. The rocking of the boat. Did he feel sea-sick? He'd been warned that he might. No, not sick exactly. Just dazed. A queer rhythm going on inside him, back and forth, back and forth. Or was it up and down, up and down? It was a weird, swooping mixture of the two. It made him feel different . . .unreal . . . .

So he'd left his parents in the bar and come up on deck, even though all was grey and misty and there was a fleck of rain in the air. No one was about, at first.

He leaned on the rail and looked down into the water. Suddenly he thought of all that depth of sea beneath them. Suppose they sank! Nonsense. Channel steamers didn't sink—

'I hope she's sunk all right,' said a voice behind him. A booming sort of voice, like a distant fog-horn.

Startled, he turned to see a tall man with a big black beard and moustache. 'Seen my wife?' the man asked.

'Er – no – I haven't seen anyone,' said Jack.

'Oh. Good. I expect she's sunk all right then, I was afraid she might have bobbed up, like a balloon.' Blackbeard peered over the side, into the murky water. 'No sign, thank goodness,' he said. 'Didn't really think there would be, but you never know with a persistent woman like Annabel.'

'Annabel?' echoed Jack.

'My wife. Couldn't stand her any longer. Brought her on this boat for a trip to the other side. Pushed her overboard. Felt a bit sea-sick afterwards. Rested in the cabin. Then I was suddenly scared in case she'd bobbed up. No. No sign of her. Whew!'

He brought out a large grey handkerchief and mopped his brow, nose, cheeks, beard, moustache and eyes, then he smiled at Jack.

'Never get married, young man,' he said.

'I don't think I ever would,' Jack responded seriously. 'I don't care much for females. They seem unnatural, somehow.'

'Unnatural. Never said a truer word,' agreed Blackbeard. 'Their minds don't work, that's the trouble. They have feelings. All these emotions, perceptions, imaginings. Before I brought her on board, my wife said: "You're going to try to get rid of me. I feel it in my bones." Well, how could she know? Unnatural. But I did more than try. I *have* got rid of her. I hope.' He looked over the side again. 'Yes, she must have well and truly sunk by now. Fat woman. Do you know why wives are fat while girl friends are slim?'

Jack shook his head.

'Because wives relax, boy. They've got their man.

They're secure for life. They have an income without work. Take Annabel. Beautiful girl when she was young. Loved her.'

Tears suddenly filled his eyes and rolled down into his moustache and beard, so that his face in the greyness shone with mingled tears and rain. 'Yes, loved her once. Really did!'

'Why?' asked Jack.

'Why? She was lively, affectionate, aimed to please. But once she had a ring on her finger and a house to sit in, she just sat. Sat and ate sweets and read novels and watched telly. She sat and grew fat and she always wore black. Said she was "in mourning for her life". That's a quote from some Russian play she'd seen on telly. She said I had no soul. Well, I *had* to get rid of her.'

'A man's gotta do what a man's gotta do,' said Jack, quoting a recent telly advert.

'Exactly,' said Blackbeard, with a sigh.

Jack said, 'You are pulling my leg, aren't you? I mean – you didn't really push her overboard.'

'Of course I did,' fog-horned the man. 'What else are we talking about? I wanted to be free!'

'I like to be free, too,' agreed Jack, 'but I wouldn't drown anyone to be it. It's not right to kill people, even if they're a nuisance. Suppose she comes back and haunts you.'

'Annabel, a ghost? Ever heard of a *fat* ghost? No . . .' And at that moment a huge blackness seemed to form itself out of the nothingness of the mist, and a woman's voice said: 'Is that you, Gregory?'

Blackbeard jumped so much that he nearly went over the side.

'Annabel!' he gasped. 'But you're dead!'

'So are you,' said the fat woman in black. She had

a sweet, delicate voice. 'I poisoned your drink before you drowned me. You're lying dead in our cabin at this moment, only you're so insensitive you don't realise it.' She turned to Jack. 'Hello, little boy. Can you see us?'

Jack nodded.

'Really? Dear child, you must be psychic. Gregory, it'll be interesting for us to wander around and find out who sees us and who doesn't. We can separate the sensitives from the clodhoppers.'

'How did you get out of the water?' demanded her husband.

'I didn't. That is, my body didn't. But *I'm* here. You really *are* dead, Gregory, otherwise you wouldn't be able to see me. *You're* not psychic. You have no more spirituality than a pudding. If you don't believe me, go along to the cabin and see for yourself.'

'I did lie down in the cabin, feeling sick, after I'd drowned you,' the man admitted. 'It was a shock to my system. I remembered some of the old, happy times, before the rot set in. Then I pulled myself together and came up here.'

'You pulled yourself together and came out of your body, dear, just as I did,' said his wife. 'Go down to the cabin and take a look at your old self.'

'Oh, all right – just to prove you wrong.' Blackbeard vanished.

The woman turned to Jack. 'Are Gregory and I the first ghosts you've ever met?' she asked chattily.

'Guess so,' muttered Jack – not that he believed for one minute that either of them was a ghost, but he thought it best to humour them. 'What did you poison your husband with?' he asked in the same chatty tone as the woman.

'Weed-killer,' she answered with a chuckle.

'Suitable, eh? He looks like an odd sort of weed, with all that hair. I knew he was going to drown me, you see. I'm a very sensitive creature and I felt it in my bones. It's because I always felt things so intensely in my bones that I let myself grow fat, to protect my bones. But I went on being sensitive. Anyway, I decided that if he could be so selfish and unfriendly as to murder me, I'd do the same to him. Tit for tat. Poor Gregory. Now he's lost his own life but he hasn't lost me. We'll be bound together for all eternity, the couple who murdered each other. What closer ties? But I will try to be nicer to him now. What do you think of it all?'

'You won't like it if I tell you what I honestly think,' said Jack.

'Never mind, child. Out with it.'

'I think,' Jack said carefully, 'that the rocking of the boat and maybe quite a lot of duty-free wallop at the bar has made you and your husband have delusions. You're having a sort of shared D.T.s. That,' he explained patiently, 'is *delirium tremens*. Alcoholics have it. They see things that aren't there, like green snakes and pink elephants and whatnot, and have other peculiar experiences. You may have wanted to do each other in, but you obviously didn't or you wouldn't be here. That's what I think.'

He also thought she might be angered. Grown-ups usually resent very much being told that they're drunk, especially by a child, but she smiled at him affectionately.

'You dear little soul,' she said. 'Here you are, psychic as they make 'em, communing with ghosts, and you don't even realise it. I expect a lot of people you've talked to during your life have been ghosts, and you simply haven't known. You must take notice next time you bump into someone and feel nothing – or shake hands with someone, and find yourself grasping thin air.'

She sighed, and a cool wind blew. 'Do you know what I'm going to miss most now I'm a ghost?'

'The telly?'

'Oh, no. I can still watch that. I'll be invisible to most people, so I can walk into any living-room and join the family. Maybe the dog will growl or the cat's fur will stand on end or the room will turn chilly, but no one will know it's me. No, what I shall miss is eating. I've really enjoyed eating, since I was married and could let my looks go. Gregory likes his grub, too. He'll miss eating. We'll have that in common. A shared loss.'

'But it'll be convenient,' said Jack, joining in her "game" again instead of being sceptical. 'If you don't need food, you won't need money. Everything will be free.'

'That's true. We shall be able to travel the world without needing any food to sustain us, and without paying any fares. Yes, it'll be lovely. We'll travel for the rest of our lives.'

'Lives? If you're both dead?' said Jack sharply.

'Don't you try to catch me out, young man. The afterlife is as much a life as the one you've got. I don't know everything about it yet as I'm still a "new girl", but I'm finding my way around.'

Blackbeard appeared suddenly. He grinned. 'Our cabin is empty,' he said. 'No body.'

'That's nothing,' said Annabel. 'It only means that the steward found it while we were talking here and had you put wherever they do put dead bodies on board ship.'

'Where would that be?' Jack asked, fascinated.

'I don't know,' she said. 'Gregory and I can go on an invisible walk-about later and find what they've done with him. In the old slave ships they used to put dead slaves in the cooking-pot to feed the crew. Perhaps the Captain will be having a fry-up of Gregory's kidneys for breakfast. I'd quite fancy that myself, with some bacon and a tomato – and butter and marmalade and toast—'

'Trust you to think of nothing but your stomach, even when you're dead!' blazed Gregory, then made a superhuman effort to control his irritation. 'Annabel, please understand that you *are* dead now – dead as mutton – dead as a door-nail – dead as the dodo —'

'Perhaps we'll meet a dodo on our travels,' his wife said dreamily.

'–and therefore,' Blackbeard continued, 'you have no right to be here. It's not suitable. Dead people are supposed to lie down —'

'But you didn't, Gregory, and we're in the same boat. Where shall we go then?' She looked at Jack. 'Any suggestions?'

'I suggest,' said Jack, deciding at this moment that whatever work he took up in life he would not be a mental nurse or warden of a home for alcoholics, 'that you go to the bar and have a cup of strong black coffee together – and make friends.'

'Isn't he sweet?' said Annabel. 'He still doesn't believe that we're ghosts.'

'You've had a jolly good fight,' said Jack, 'drowning and poisoning each other, or pretending to, and now it's time to make up and be friends. Please! It would be – well – nice,' he concluded feebly.

Husband and wife regarded each other.

'He's right,' said Annabel. 'It would be nice. We'll be together for ever now, Gregory, so let's be friends. I apologise for poisoning you with weed-killer.'

'Now you apologise to her for whatever you did,' said Jack.

'I apologise for drowning you,' muttered Blackbeard. 'I *was* sorry afterwards, actually.'

'Now shake hands,' said Jack.

They did, and Annabel said: 'Place your hands on ours, to give us your blessing.'

Jack tried to do so, but the boat lurched at that moment so he didn't actually touch the clasped hands.

'Oh, I do feel peculiar,' said Blackbeard, in the tone of a bewildered fog-horn.

'So do I, love, but we'll soon get accustomed,' said Annabel.

'I feel a bit sick, too. Excuse me,' said Jack, and left them standing together at the rail. Cor! he thought. A right couple of loonies. But interesting. Leaves you with something to think about.

He walked on another part of the deck until his sickish feeling wore off, then began to make his way to the bar to rejoin his parents. As he passed a door marked MEDICAL ROOM, a man with a stethoscope round his neck – apparently a doctor – was just coming out and saying to another man: 'It wasn't ordinary sea-sickness. People don't die of that, although they often feel as if they're dying. Food-poisoning, more like.' And just for a second Jack wondered if Annabel's tale of poisoning were true, and those two had been ghosts, and he really was psychic. He tried bumping into a few people to see if he felt anything. He felt the bumps all right. So did his victims – 'Look where you're going, lad! My corns are not for stamping on!'

At last he reached his parents at their table in the bar.

'Feeling seedy, darling? You're very pale,' said his

mother. 'It is rather a rough crossing.'

'You can say that again,' said Jack.

His father brought him a glass of lemonade and he sat there sipping it. Everything settled back into a kind of normality. He even wondered if he'd dreamed those two people on deck. All this rocking and swaying did make one light-headed. Perhaps he'd imagined the whole incident —

Then the door of the bar swung open and the mysterious couple, Blackbeard and his wife, walked in, large as life and arm-in-arm. They didn't look at all drunk – and they'd made friends. Jack felt he'd had some share in that and, when they smiled and waved to him, he smiled and waved back. They went to sit at a table some distance away, but didn't order anything.

'Who were you waving to?' asked his mother.

'The couple that's just sat down over there. I met them on deck. They'd had a bit of a tiff but they're O.K. now.'

He returned his empty lemonade glass to the counter and, as he did so, heard one of the assistants say to the other: 'Rough old crossing in more senses than one. A Mr Gregory Lake has died of food-poisoning, and his wife is missing, presumed drowned.'

Can't be the same as my couple, thought Jack, giving another wave and smile to his friends. But they were absorbed in each other now, holding hands across the table – and she seemed to be slimmer than before, and prettier – and he looked younger and his beard was less aggressive —

His mother asked: 'Jack, who do you keep waving to?'

'That couple – I told you – at that table.' He pointed.

'But that table,' said his mother, 'is empty.'

Jack went cold and whispered: 'Are you sure?'

'Of course I'm sure. What's the matter with you?'

'I'm psychic,' said Jack, with wonder and a touch of pride.

'Sea-sick, more like,' said his father. 'Never mind, Jack, boy. We'll soon be on the other side. It's like another world over there.'

True enough, the ship was approaching the shore and the mist had cleared. They came out of it as if it had been a dream. They went to the rail to watch the land approach.

And suddenly Jack saw two figures who were going to reach the other side before the ship made port. They were walking, or floating, rather, ahead of the ship. They looked absurd, yet touching at the same time, the rather plump woman in black and the tall bearded man, hand-in-hand, skimming across the water . . .

They're in love again, Jack thought proudly, and I 'brought them together'. But he was congratulating himself a bit too soon for, as he watched, the outline of the two figures became rather less lovey-dovey. Annabel looked as if she'd given Gregory a pretty sharp kick on the ankle – and he'd kicked her back. The two heads turned towards each other, in obvious argument.

What were they saying?

A seagull shrilled across the sky. Through its cry, Jack heard Annabel's voice: 'I am being nice – nice – nice – nice —' and through the noise of a distant fog-horn came Gregory's angry: 'Oh, you – you – you – you – YOU!'

The Man Who Hated Children

adapted by Peter Eldin
from a television play
by Brian Patten

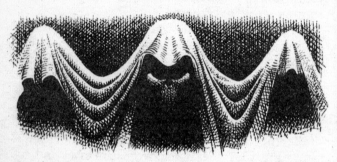

As consciousness slowly dawned, Councillor Higgs looked angrily around the room in an attempt to discover what had awakened him from his slumber in mid-snore. The sound of laughter rustled in through the window – children's laughter, happy laughter.

'Hmmph!' grunted Higgs as he rolled out of bed to land in a flabby heap on the floor. 'Darn kids. It shouldn't be allowed.'

Like a cat stalking an unsuspecting mouse, Higgs crept stealthily across the floor towards the window. With a sudden burst of energy and uttering a triumphant war cry he grabbed an old boot from a pile kept beneath the window for this particular purpose. Swiftly he opened the window and hurled the boot out, narrowly missing one of the children below.

As they scattered, Councillor Higgs chortled to

himself and prepared for the next round in the battle. He knew what those horrible kids would do next. They would throw the boot back in through the open window but Higgs would be ready for them. Picking up a cricket bat he had confiscated, he stood and faced the window in a classic batting pose – and then he waited.

In the street below Tom and Willie were about to throw the boot back as Higgs expected. But this time they had something extra in mind.

'Do you think the plan will work?' asked Tom anxiously. 'It seems ages since he confiscated my cricket bat.'

Willie nodded, 'Of course it'll work.'

He picked up a stink bomb and held it against the boot whilst Tom used a strip of sellotape to hold it in position.

'Hey, be careful with them,' said Willie. 'I don't want to go home stinking.'

When all the stink bombs were eventually in position on the boot, the two boys sat back to admire their work.

'I hope it works,' said Tom. 'He might not hit it back this time.'

Willie looked at him in disgust. 'Of course it'll work. He always hits it back. It's become a kind of ritual with him. Captain Higgs of the Loony Eleven . . . beaten by the atomic stink boot bomb!'

Almost in unison each boy removed a grubby handkerchief from his pocket, folded it diagonally, then tied it around his nose and mouth, and walked towards the window.

'Higgsie! Higgsie! Higgsie! Here's your boot back Piggy Higgsie!'

A gleam of self satisfaction entered Higgs's eyes and he gripped the handle of the cricket bat with increased determination. A cry of 'Geronimo!' from outside warned him that the boot was on its way. Seconds later, true to form, the boot came sailing in through the window.

One hit – and Higgs staggered under the impact of a foul smell.

Holding his nose in one hand and the bat in the other he careered around the room moaning and groaning. The smell was obviously coming from the cricket bat. He staggered towards the window and threw the bat out.

'You're a genius, Willie,' said Tom as he moved forward to pick up the bat.

The bat retrieved, the two boys ran for their lives as they were assailed by a barrage of old boots. When they looked back they saw Higgs jumping up and down furiously, shouting and waving his fist at them. But as one hand was still over his nose and mouth to keep out the foul stench of the stink bombs the boys could not hear what he was saying. Which was just as well.

'Remember, you're sworn to secrecy about this place, Tom,' said Willie as he counted along the boards of a wooden fence. 'One, two, three, four, five, six. This is the one. We'll hide the cricket bat here until the stink wears off.' They squeezed through the fence into an overgrown garden. It was like a jungle, only a little more friendly.

Willie replaced the special plank and they ventured further into what had once been a fine garden. Now the roses, lilies and rhododendrons were fighting a losing battle against the weeds. Ahead of them lay a combed-down path through the undergrowth that Willie had made on previous visits.

Having hidden the bat under the porch steps of a

ruined building they returned the way they had come, and made their exit into the outside world. They wandered on to school laughing and congratulating themselves on their victory over Councillor Higgs.

The doors of the Committee Room opened with all the pomp and ceremony the local town hall could muster and in marched the committee – each man a proud and reliable member of the community with a sense of purpose, dedication, and duty. Each took his seat at the large table, until only one chair remained empty.

Twenty-five seconds later Councillor Higgs arrived. The other members could almost set their watches by him. He always arrived twenty-five seconds late in order to make an impressive entrance. 'Good morning, gentlemen!'

At the head of the table the Chairman waited while Higgs took his seat, and then opened the proceedings. 'Two things on the agenda this morning, gentlemen. The first is the business with the gardens. As you are aware, we have to decide whether or not to approve and finance the new playground. And secondly . . . a rather different project. Would you like to explain it Mason? Mason!'

Mason, the oldest member of the council, had dozed off – but at the sound of his name, a sound not often heard in the Committee Room, he suddenly came to life. After a short fumble in his pocket he managed to produce a wallet. More fumbling was followed by the production from the wallet of a photograph which was then passed round the table as Mason began his carefully prepared speech. For a whole week he had practised this speech in front of his children, his wife, the mirror, the dog, and the budgie and now his big moment had come.

'When I was a child I was befriended by a rather famous playwright called Sir James Barrie. I'm sure you have heard of him, gentlemen.' There was little reaction, apart from a snort or two from Higgs. He continued regardless. 'Please be careful with that photograph, gentlemen, for it is rather precious to me. It was taken in Kensington Gardens. You will no doubt recall that James Barrie wrote the book *Peter Pan* and . . . .' Another disgusted snort from Higgs '. . . and I distinctly remember him showing me two peculiar stones in the garden. On one were the initials P.P. and on the other was the single letter W. Legend has it that they are the magic stones of Peter Pan and Wendy.'

At this point the remembrance of the occasion was just a little too much for Mr Mason and he had to stop his discourse to blow his nose.

'One day I went back to the gardens to try and locate the stones again . . . but they had gone.'

A barrage of complete uninterest pervaded the room. At this point, the Chairman decided that it was time to intervene. He coughed, and rustled the papers in his briefcase, a signal that he was about to take part in the discussion.

'At the time a Mr Heronymous Higgs was chairman of the local council,' said the Chairman.

'A great man. Great man,' mumbled Higgs and then added, as if it was just an afterthought, 'he was a relation of mine.'

The Chairman ignored Higgs and continued, 'And it was at Mr Heronymous Higgs's instigation that the stones were removed and placed elsewhere. Unfortunately their present whereabouts is unknown.'

Seeing that his plea was getting nowhere fast,

Mason chipped in. 'Those stones are part of local history. Whoever stands on or near to the stones can make a wish and it will come true!'

Higgs had now received the ageing photograph. It showed a very blurred and highly tinted picture of an adult and a child standing beside two small stones.

He snorted. 'Rubbish, balderdash. Peter Pan, magic, I never heard such nonsense in my life. P.P. stands for Parish of Paddington and as for W. well, that's probably for Waterworks or Westminster, certainly not Wendy.' With that, he collapsed into paroxysms of laughter.

Once again the Chairman thought it time to smooth matters over. 'The point is, gentlemen, we would like to find these stones and restore them to the park if this is possible. It would add a little local colour.'

Higgs glowered with distaste at the Chairman. Leaning to his left, where his old crony Sliggs was seated, he whispered, 'We'll convince them of their folly. Pampering to revolting childish whims. First playgrounds for those ghastly children and now magic stones, it's ludicrous. You're with me aren't you, Sliggs? If you want to retain a place on this committee when I become Chairman . . . ?'

Sliggs humbly nodded his agreement.

'Good,' said Higgs. 'Come to my house, early this evening. I have a plan.'

That evening, Higgs and his partner-in-crime, Sliggs, prepared to implement Higgs's anti-children campaign. Higgs picked up a gun and placed it into a sack along with several other items.

'That's a bit drastic, isn't it Higgs?' queried Sliggs who was beginning to have second thoughts.

'Nonsense!' said Higgs. 'It's only a toy. All these

toys are essential to my plan. We'll plunder a few flowerbeds, break a few branches, and then scatter these toys around as evidence.'

'But where did you get this stuff?' asked Sliggs.

'Thrown at me by young vandals!'

'Even this?' exclaimed Sliggs, picking up a skateboard.

'Yes, even that,' replied Higgs. 'And this plastic duck was thrown forcibly at me from a pram several years ago by . . . .' He was interrupted in midsentence by the sound of giggling. 'Hush, did you hear something?' With an agility born of years of practice Higgs swiftly turned off the light and tiptoed across the room. As he reached the window he groped automatically for one of the old boots. But he had used the last that morning.

'Come on,' he cried to Sliggs, grabbing two Mickey Mouse masks from the table. 'I think we've got 'em.'

Tom and Willie were hurrying home from the park already late for supper, when suddenly from out of a dark side alley leapt two figures wearing Mickey Mouse masks.

Tom froze in his tracks, Willie tried to run, but soon they were both overpowered. Higgs searched Willie and found a packet of initialled pens in his inside pocket.

'Just the thing!' said Higgs gleefully and proceeded to drag Willie to a nearby hut into which he was promptly locked along with Tom.

'Good work, eh, Sliggs?' said Higgs as they re-entered the house. 'I've been after those horrors for a long time.'

But Sliggs was beginning to feel that things were getting just a little out of hand. 'I'm a bit nervous about all this, Higgs. It does seem a bit drastic.

Kidnapping those two boys and then sneaking about the park in the dead of night.'

'Nonsense,' replied Higgs. 'Everything is working perfectly. We'll let them out later. Nobody will believe them against us and if they're late home – well it'll soon be well known what they'd been doing! You can't back out now, Sliggs. It's important work we are doing. Come on, to the park, with a vengeance!'

'One, two, three, four, five, six.' Willie counted along the planks, found the loose one, and the two boys slipped into the old garden.

'I wonder what Higgs is up to? Why steal my pens – and your bus pass, then lock us up in that shed – what are they up to?'

'We could have been there all night if you hadn't found that loose board,' said Tom. 'You're a regular Houdini, Willie.'

But Willie wasn't listening. He was already heading through the undergrowth. 'Hey, wait for me,' called Tom a little apprehensively as he ran to catch up with his friend.

When Tom reached the broken, creeper-covered building, Willie was sitting on the steps deep in thought. Tom removed the cricket bat from its hiding place. 'Still smells,' he said and began tearing up some grass near Willie's feet to clean the bat.

'Something else smells, as well,' said Willie thoughtfully. 'Creepy Higgs and Slimy Sliggs — they're up to something. They're definitely up to something.'

'Well,' said Tom, who was now busily engaged in cleaning the bat with the grass he had torn up. 'If they are, there's not much we can do about it. When grown-ups do something wrong, you can't tell other grown-ups, can you. Because the only way we usually find out that they're doing something wrong is by doing something wrong ourselves, like spying or breaking windows. And then it's us that gets told off and then . . . Well, it's not fair is it?'

But Willie, who was on his feet now, was not really listening. 'I wish . . .' He stopped in mid-thought. It seemed as if the evening had suddenly become alive. The birds appeared to be singing louder than before. A slight breeze began whistling through the trees. There was a feeling of electricity in the air.

Tom sensed it too and looked round apprehensively. 'What – what do you wish for, Willie?'

Willie looked down at him as if he had just come out of a trance. 'Oh – nothing really. I was just wishing that someone would help us deal with Higgs and Sliggs. Come on let's go home – it's getting late.'

Tom hurriedly returned the bat to its hiding place. As he did so its tip hit the stone upon which Willie had been standing. It bore the initials P.P. They left by the fence and made their way home.

Inside the garden the breeze had been transformed into a light wind. As it whistled through the trees it seemed that the lilt of pipes could be heard.

Two strange beings, dressed in old clothes and wearing Mickey Mouse masks, crept on hands and knees through the bushes of Kensington Gardens. A particularly sharp stone penetrated the flesh of the one at the rear and brought him quickly to a pained halt. He looked at his watch and a desperate expression fell over his face behind the jovial mask.

'Don't you think this is a bit dramatic, Higgs?' he whispered.

'Shush!' came the anxious reply as a park policeman rode past on a bike, singing merrily to himself. The two men waited in the bushes in silence for what seemed an interminable age. Sliggs's knees were sore and damp. He wished he hadn't come.

In the near distance they heard a cycle bell. Then came the clanging of gates.

'That's it!' said Higgs triumphantly. 'The park's closed. Have you got the sack and the shears?'

'Yes. But I didn't think we'd need shears, Higgs. I thought we'd just pluck, as it were, a few flowers . . .'

'Pah!' snorted Higgs. 'I was thinking more in terms of uprooting the rose bushes they've planted around the statue of that horrid child.'

Sliggs gulped. Events seemed to be getting a little out of hand. 'You mean . . .'

'Yes,' interrupted Higgs, 'I mean that Peter Pan statue. It's perverted you know, Sliggs. Putting up statues of children in the parks. It just encourages them.'

Higgs began moving forward, eager to get started. Sliggs slouched unwillingly behind. 'But isn't it a bit extreme to rip up rose bushes, Higgs?'

'Rose bushes and children have nothing in common,' said Higgs loudly. 'They smell completely different.' It was obvious to Sliggs that that particular conversation was at an end but as they crept forward in the dark he had a strange feeling that they were being watched.

Higgs, too, in spite of all his previous confidence, was beginning to feel that there was something wrong. Something he couldn't put his finger on. More of an intuition than anything concrete. Eventually the feeling got the better of him and he turned to Sliggs.

'Are there animals in this park, Sliggs?'

'Animals . . .?'

'Wild animals,' added Higgs.

'There are some ducks, Higgs,' replied Sliggs – a feeling of doubt entered his mind. 'Higgs, ducks aren't very ferocious . . . are they, Higgs?' But Higgs had already vanished into the bushes.

Then a short distance away, he heard the sound of a bush being attacked and Higgs's maniacal giggling. When Sliggs eventually found his colleague a sight of absolute devastation met his eyes. Higgs had already broken several branches from one of the bushes and was now hard at work trying to pull a rose bush out by its roots.

'I say, Higgs. Nobody would believe little children did that,' said Sliggs.

'Of course they will,' replied Higgs gleefully. 'Especially if I leave some toys around. Soon as we've finished here we'll make an anonymous call to the police.' He set to work pulling up another rose bush. 'We'll say we saw some children climbing over the park railings with malicious intent in their eyes.'

Sliggs was not so keen on the idea and was frantically trying to replace the uprooted flowers as fast as Higgs was pulling them out. 'But . . . I think . . . Perhaps . . . What if . . . Maybe . . .'

But Higgs was enjoying himself immensely. 'A perfect situation,' he said. 'We scarper, let those two brats out of the shed. The police will put one and one together and it'll make . . . by Jove, Sliggs, it'll make the headlines! "*Child Vandals!*".' He took the sack from Sliggs, opened it and removed a pen, a bus pass, a yellow plastic duck, and some other items which he dumped among the uprooted flowers.

Sliggs was unable to take all this in one go. Luckily he had brought his hip flask with him and he took a quick, reassuring swig of whisky. And then another. And then another.

'Right, now we'll be off. Go separate ways but be careful when you climb out over the railings. I'll 'phone the police from a callbox in Queensgate. You'd better call for me tomorrow morning. We'll walk to work together. And Sliggs . . .?'

'Yes?' said the bewildered Sliggs.

'Mum's the word, Sliggs.' And with a cheery wave Higgs crawled off into the darkness.

Sliggs surveyed the damage all around him – and took another swig of whisky. He had just removed the hip flask from his lips when he heard music. Pipe music floating through the air. He went to run but was stopped in his tracks. One of the flowers had moved!

He looked again.

Yes, it had moved, and now the other uprooted flowers were moving in time with the music and replanting themselves in their former positions. The rose bushes moved back to their places and the soil fell magically into place around their roots. Sliggs gazed open-mouthed in amazement, he could not believe his eyes. He took another swig.

'I hate that statue,' said a child's voice.

Sliggs reeled around. Now what was happening? He decided to investigate and staggered off drunkenly in the direction from which the voice had come. He crawled through the bushes until he reached an open area near the pool where he stopped for another gulp from his flask. He looked around apprehensively but everything was quiet and peaceful in the golden moonlight.

'Must have been my imagination,' he thought. And then he heard the voice again.

'Oh, it might be a good statue as far as statues go; but honestly, does it look a bit like me?'

Sliggs moved stealthily forward and peered through the bushes. A short distance away he saw a swan floating near the bank. 'Nothing unusual in that,' thought Sliggs but he almost fell into the water in amazement when the swan spoke.

'It's an idealised version of you. You know what human beings are like.'

'It's sissy!' replied the voice.

Sliggs peered in the direction from which the voice had come. There on the bank was a small, almost naked, boy. An impish, rather tubby person sitting calmly by the water's edge, his chin cupped in his hands, chatting to the swan. 'Peter Pan!' thought Sliggs instinctively.

'The fairies look all right on the statue,' said the boy. 'Tell me about them again, Mr Swan.'

'Well,' replied the swan. 'When the first baby in the world smiled, its smile broke into a million pieces, and each piece became a fairy.'

'Do you really believe that?' said Peter Pan, who was now happily dangling his legs in the water.

'No, not in the slightest, but it's what they say.' And with that the swan shook its wings and glided away.

Sliggs, his eyes as large as saucers, had seen enough. Clambering to his feet he turned away and staggered back through the park. Only the repeated sounds of his hiccups fading into the distance broke the stillness of the night air.

The following morning Sliggs walked slowly and reluctantly to Higgs's house. He had no idea how he was going to tell Higgs what had happened in the park after he had left. No doubt he would not believe him anyway. And he had a splitting headache caused by all that whisky.

Higgs was already at the window. He had heard

Sliggs approaching and thought it might be children. And he had managed to find one old boot . . . he was a little disappointed at missing a chance to throw the boot at some little brat.

'Morning, Sliggs. A good night's work, eh? Got away safely then did you?'

Sliggs groaned, still clutching his head.

'I'm not up to this sort of thing.' He staggered into the room and slumped into a chair as Higgs began to flop into his morning exercises.

'Everything went according to plan,' said Higgs gleefully. 'The brats had escaped but I made the 'phone call to the police – said they'd investigate immediately. Ha!' He breathed out heavily as though convincing himself that the exercises were doing him some good. 'Ha!' came another expellation of air as he stood up after trying to touch his toes. Unfortunately he could not see his toes below the bulge of his stomach but he knew they must be there somewhere.

'They wanted to know my name and all that,' he said, now red-faced and flustered as he tried, rather unsuccessfully, to complete one press-up. 'I said I was a citizen going about his business. Clever, eh, Sliggs – clever.'

Perhaps now was a good time to mention what had happened, thought Sliggs. 'Er, last night Higgs . . . last night I saw a swan . . .'

'A swan?'

'Yes, a swan and a boy, talking about fairies . . . and . . . and . . .'

Higgs had finished his morning exercises and was now dressing himself, stopping every ten seconds or so to admire his corpulent frame in the mirror.

'Fairies? Fairies – you drink too much Sliggs. That's your trouble. Come on. We'll walk across the park and see our night's work. That will clear your head.'

When they arrived at the Peter Pan statue Higgs looked eagerly for signs of his handiwork. First he glared in disbelief at the neat rows of healthy plants and then his disbelief turned to anger, aimed at Sliggs.

'Traitor! You stuck them back when I left last night. You deliberately stuck them back in the ground. That's ruined your chances on the committee I can tell you.'

'I . . . I didn't, Higgs, honestly I didn't.'

Higgs's anger was now positively at boiling point – he rushed across the garden and began tugging at a bush. 'Then it was the brats after they'd got out of the shed. They must have replanted the bushes and taken the toys.'

'No, no, Higgs, it was . . .' he began to plead but was stopped in mid-sentence as he spotted a swan gliding across the water towards them.

Higgs, too, had spotted something – a policeman. 'We'd better act normally. I think we're being watched,' he whispered, keeping an eye on the policeman.

'Yes, I think you're right,' whispered Sliggs, keeping an eye on the swan.

Willie lifted the sixth plank and the two boys entered the old garden. When they reached the ruined house they saw a pile of toys and the things that Higgs had taken from them. They moved forward slowly, wondering how they had got there. Willie was the first to dare to pick something up. It was Tom's bus pass. He looked at it quizzically and then handed it to Tom. His pens were there as well. He picked them up and dropped them into his pocket.

'Hello!' said Willie as he spotted the yellow plastic duck. 'That's strange after all this time. I lost it years ago when I was little. I think someone stole it from me. And this . . .' he picked up a model car, ' . . . it's ages since I saw this.'

'Do you think someone put it all here? Perhaps Creepy Higgs and Slimy Sliggs.'

Almost simultaneously the same thought hit the two boys. 'The bat!' They rushed across to the hiding place under the steps and heaved a double sigh of relief.

Tom was now beginning to get a little scared at this strange turn of events. 'Do you think it was them, Willie?' he said. 'Do you think they know about this place?'

'Dunno,' replied Willie thoughtfully, 'But it's very strange. I mean why would Higgs give us our toys back – he hates kids.' A strange lilting music began rippling through the trees but the boys were too engrossed to notice. 'I just wish he'd change into something . . . anything.'

The music started playing again – this time the boys heard it.

'What's that?' asked Willie.

'Oh, it's just the wind,' explained Tom, trying to convince himself as well as Willie. 'But this place gives me the creeps. Come on, let's go.'

As they reached the fence Tom kicked a tin can into the garden to show he was not afraid of a little wind rustling through the trees. The can sailed through the air and hit a stone with a clang.

It was the stone bearing the initials P.P.

Higgs paced up and down his room, deep in thought. 'There must be a logical explanation, Sliggs.' And he paced up and down some more.

Then it dawned on him. 'Deep roots. That's what it is. The flowers were deeply rooted. Ha! Simple!'

Sliggs began to protest. 'But Higgs, you plucked . . . .'

'A saw! Ha! I need a saw!' said Higgs, oblivious to his colleague's protestations.

'But we did snip . . .'

'For a tree,' continued Higgs. Sliggs looked horrified at the thought but Higgs was too enraptured with his fiendish idea to notice. 'Yes, I need a saw for a tree. We'll saw down a tree!'

'I've gone off the whole idea completely, Higgs,' wailed Sliggs.

But Higgs was well away. 'I can see the headlines already – "*Young vandals cut down oak trees*" . . .'

'Trees!' thought Sliggs anxiously. It had been a tree a few seconds ago, now it was plural. Before long Higgs would have the whole park demolished. 'I'll have nothing to do with it,' he said . . . and he continued saying it all the way to the park.

'There's a good 'un,' shouted Higgs heading for a majestic oak, saw at the ready.

Sliggs looked anxiously around. Nearby a car hooted – and he almost had a heart attack. A few seconds later a duck quacked – and Sliggs nearly jumped out of his skin. He wished he'd brought his hip flask.

'Stop pussyfooting about!' Higgs called to the dithering Sliggs. 'Make yourself useful. Scatter a few marbles in the grass.'

Sliggs removed some marbles from his pocket and began scattering them half-heartedly on the ground. 'It's not very subtle,' he said.

'Of course its subtle,' said Higgs.

'Not the marbles. I mean its not subtle cutting down a tree. Higgs . . . Higgs, that tree probably took a hundred years to grow to its present height.'

But Higgs was not listening. He was beginning to saw the tree and he was so engrossed in his dastardly deed he did not even notice the pipe music wafting by on the breeze.

Sliggs heard it and ran to a nearby bush for protection. The moon vanished behind a dark cloud and Sliggs shivered in the bush. The music seemed to be getting closer.

Then from out of the darkness Sliggs heard a sickly groan. 'Sliggs. Something's happening to me, Sliggs.'

As the moon came out again, Sliggs saw his companion once more. Something certainly was happening. He had dropped the saw and was now standing motionless.

'I can't move my feet,' stammered Higgs who was getting rather scared.

Sliggs looked at his friend's feet. As he watched, transfixed in amazement, roots appeared from Higgs's shoes and trouser legs. 'Higgs!' screamed Sliggs so loudly that his voice could be heard above the music. 'Higgs, you've got roots in your boots!'

Higgs tried to look down but his whole body was beginning to stiffen. Branches and leaves began sprouting out of him. He tried to yell, but it was hopeless.

Sliggs stumbled across to the saw and picked it up. He staggered round and round his friend, who now looked more like a tree than a human being, moaning and groaning.

From the other side of the bushes there emerged a bluff, moustachioed policeman. 'Evening, Sir. A bit late to be in the park isn't it?' Then he noticed the saw and the marks on the oak tree. Now another – a new tree – stood next to it, but policemen do not go round counting trees. He just frowned at the saw cuts and turned back to Sliggs who was babbling like a madman about music, and Peter Pan, and swans, and trees . . . 'Do you mind explaining this?' said the policeman pointing to the damaged tree, 'and I'll have the saw, sir, if you don't mind.'

Sliggs paid no attention as the policeman took the saw. He just continued muttering excitedly to himself, staring wide-eyed at the new tree.

'I think you'd better come along with me, sir,' said the policeman and he forcibly assisted Sliggs out of the park.

Higgs watched the scene through his foliage but there was nothing he could do. There were now branches where his hands had once been, knots formed in place of his eyes, nose and mouth . . . his skin had turned to bark.

'I hope those rotten kids don't try and saw me down,' he thought.

The House that Lacked a Bogle

Sorche Nic Leodhas

There once was a house that lacked a bogle. That would be no great thing for a house to be wanting in the ordinary way, but it happened that this house was in St Andrews. That being a town where every one of the best houses has a ghost or a bogle, as they call it, of its own, or maybe two or even more, the folk who lived in the house felt the lack sorely. They were terribly ashamed when their friends talked about their bogles, seeing that they had none of their own.

The worst of it was that they had but lately come into money and had bought the house to set themselves up in the world. They never thought to ask if it had a bogle when they bought it, just taking it for granted that it had. But what good was it to be having a fine big house if there was no bogle in it? In St Andrews, anyway!

The man of the house could be reckoned a warm man with a tidy lot of money at his banker's, while his neighbour MacParlan had a hard time of it scraping enough to barely get by. But the MacParlans had

67

a bogle that had been in the family since the time of King Kenneth the First, and they had papers to prove it.

The woman of the house had two horses to her carriage, and Mrs MacNair had no carriage at all. But the MacNairs had *three* bogles, being well supplied, and Mrs MacNair was so set up about them that it fair put one's teeth on edge to hear her going on about them and their doings.

Tammas, the son of the house, told his parents that he couldn't hold up his head when chaps talked about their bogles at his school, and he had to admit that there weren't any at his house at all.

And then there was Jeannette, the daughter of the house (her name was really Janet but she didn't like the sound of it, it being so plain). Well, *she* came home one day, and banged the door to, and burst into tears. And when they all asked her what was amiss, she said she'd been humiliated entirely because they hadn't a bogle, and she'd never show her face outside the house again until her papa got one for her.

Well, it all came to this. Without a bogle, they could cut no figure at all in society, for all their money.

They did what they could, of course, to set the matter right. In fact, each one of them tried in his own way, but not letting on to the others, however, lest they be disappointed if naught came of it.

The man of the house kept an eye on MacParlan's house and found out that MacParlan's bogle liked to take a stroll by nights on the leads of MacParlan's roof. So one night, when all the MacParlans had gone off somewhere away from home, he went over and called up to MacParlan's bogle. After a bit of havering, the man got down to the point. 'Do you not get terrible tired of haunting the same old place day in and day out?' he asked.

'What way would I be doing that?' the bogle asked, very much surprised.

'Och, 'twas just a thought I had,' said the man. 'You might be liking to visit elsewhere maybe?'

'That I would not,' said the bogle flatly.

'Och well,' said the man, 'should you e'er feel the need o' a change of scene, you'll find a warm welcome at my house any time and for as long as you're liking to stay.'

The bogle peered down at him over the edge of the roof.

'Thank you kindly,' said he, 'but I'll bide here wi' my own folks. So dinna expect me.' And with that he disappeared.

So there was naught for the man to do but go back home.

The woman of the house managed to get herself asked to the MacNairs' house for tea. She took with her a note to the MacNairs' bogles, telling them she was sure the three of them must be a bit cramped for room, what with there being so many of them and the MacNairs' house being so small. So she invited any or all of them to come over and stay at her house, where they'd find plenty of room and every comfort provided that a bogle could ever wish.

When nobody was watching, she slipped the note down behind the wainscoting in the MacNairs' drawing room, where she was sure the MacNairs' bogles would be finding it.

The MacNairs' bogles found it all right, and it surprised them. They didn't know exactly what to make of the note when they'd read it. But there was no doubt the woman meant it kindly, they said to each other. Being very polite bogles, they decided that she deserved the courtesy of an answer to the note, and since none of them was very much for writing, the least they could do was to send one of themselves to decline the invitation. The woman had paid them a call, so to speak. So one of them went to attend to it that same night.

The bogle met up with the woman of the house just as she was coming out of the linen press with a pile of fresh towels in her arms. The maids had left that day, being unwilling to remain in a house so inferior that it had no bogle to it. She'd have been startled out of her wits had she not been so glad to see the bogle.

'Och then!' said she, ''tis welcome you are entirely!'

'Thank ye kindly,' said the bogle.

'You'll be stopping here I hope?' questioned the woman eagerly.

'I'm sorry to be disappointing you,' said the bogle, 'but I'm not staying. I'm needed at home.'

'Och now,' said the woman, 'and could they not make do without you just for a month or two? Or happen even a fortnight?'

But she could see for herself that the bogle was not to be persuaded. In fact, none of them could accept her invitation. That's what the bogle had come to tell her. With their thanks, of course.

'Tis a sore thing,' complained the woman, 'what with all the money paid out for the house and all, that we have no bogle of our own. Now can you be telling me why?'

'I would not like to say,' said the bogle.

But the woman was sure he knew the reason, so she pressed him until at last the bogle said reluctantly, 'Well, this is the way of it. The house is too young! Losh! 'Tis not anywhere near a hundred years old yet, and there's not been time enough for anything to have happened that would bring it a bogle of its own. And forbye . . . .' The bogle stopped talking at that point.

'Och! What more?' urged the woman.

'W-e-e-ell,' said the bogle slowly, 'I'd not be liking to hurt your feelings, but your family is not, so to speak, distinguished enough. Now you take the MacParlans and the Macphersons and the Mac-Alistairs – their families go back into the far ages. And the MacAlpines is as old as the hills and rocks and streams. As for the MacNairs,' he added proudly, 'och, well, the MacNairs *is* the MacNairs. The trouble with your family is that there is nothing of note to it. No one knows exactly where it would be belonging. There's no clan or sept o' the name. Losh! The name has not even a "Mac" at the front of it.'

'Aye,' said the woman slowly, 'I can see that fine.'

And so she could. For the truth was that they had come from Wigtown and were not a Highland family at all.

'Well,' said the bogle, 'that's the way it is. So I'll bid you good night.' And away he went like a drift of mist, leaving the poor woman of the house alone and uncomforted.

The daughter of the house had taken to her bed and spent her time there, weeping and sleeping, when she wasn't eating sweeties out of a pink satin box and reading romantic tales about lovely ladies who had adventures in castles just teeming with ghosts and handsome gentlemen in velvet suits of clothes.

So there was no one left to have a try but the son, Tammas. It must be admitted he did the best he could, even if it turned out that he was maybe a little bit too successful.

Tammas had got to the place where he kept out of

the way of his friends on account of the shame that was on the family; he being young and full of pride. He only went out by night, taking long walks in lonely places all by himself.

One night he was coming back from one of these walks, and he came along by a kirkyard. It was just the sort of spot that suited his gloomy thoughts, so he stopped and leaned over the wall to look at the long rows of gravestones.

'All those graves lying there,' he thought, 'with many a bogle from them stravaging through the town and not a one of them for us. 'Tis not fair on us.'

He stopped to think about the injustice of it, and then he said out loud, 'If there's a bogle amongst you all who's got no family of his own, let him just come along with me. He can bide with us and welcome.' And with a long, deep sigh he turned back up the road and started for home.

He'd not gone more than twenty paces past the end of the kirkyard, when of a sudden he heard a fearful noise behind him. It was so eerie that it near raised the hair right off from his head. It sounded like a cat yowling and a pig squealing and a horse neighing and an ox bellowing all at one and the same time.

Tammas scarcely dared turn and look, with the fright that was on him, but turn he did. And he saw 'twas a man coming towards him. He was dressed in Highland dress with kilt and sporran, jacket and plaid showing plain, and the moonlight glinting off his brooch and shoe buckles and off the handle of the dirk in his hose. He carried a pair of bagpipes under his arm and that was where the noise was coming from.

'Whisht, man,' called Tammas, 'leave off with the pipes now. The racket you're making's enough to wake the dead.'

''Twill do no such thing,' said the piper. 'For they're all awake already and about their business. As they should be, it being midnight.'

And he put his mouth at the pipes to give another blow.

'Och, then ye'll wake all the folks in St Andrews,' protested Tammas. 'Give over now, that's a good lad!'

'Och nay,' said the piper soothingly. 'St Andrews folk will pay us no heed. They're used to us. They even like us.'

By this time he had come up to Tammas where he stood in the middle of the road. Tammas took another look at him to see who the piper was. And losh, 'twas no man at all. 'Twas a bogle!

''Tis a strangely queer thing,' said the piper sadly. 'I've been blowin' on these things all the days of my mortal life till I plain blew the life out o' my body doing it. And I've been blowing on them two or three hundred years since then, and I just cannot learn how to play a tune on them.'

'Well, go and blow somewhere else,' Tammas told him. 'Where it's lonely, with none to hear you.'

'I'd not be liking that at all,' said the piper. 'Besides, I'm coming with you.'

'With me!' Tammas cried in alarm.

'Och aye,' said the piper, and then he added reproachfully, 'you asked me, you know. Did you not?'

'I suppose I did,' Tammas admitted reluctantly. 'But I'd no idea there'd be anyone there listening.'

'Well, *I* was there,' the piper said, 'and I was listening. I doubt that I'm the only bogle in the place without a family of my own. So I accept the invitation, and thank ye kindly. Let's be on our way.'

And off he stepped, with his kilt swinging and his arms squared just so and the pipes going at full blast.

Tammas went along with him, because there was

nowhere else he could go at that hour but back to his home.

When they got home, Tammas opened the door and into the house the two of them went. All the family came running to see what was up, for the pipes sounded worse indoors than out since there was less room there for the horrible noise to spread.

'There!' Tammas shouted at them all, raising his voice over the racket of the bagpipes. 'There's your bogle for you, and I hope you're satisfied!'

And he stamped up the stairs and into his room, where he went to bed with his pillow pulled over his ears.

Strange to tell, they really were satisfied, because now they had a bogle and could hold their own when they went out into society. Quite nicely as it happened, for they had the distinction of being the only family in the town that had a piping ghost – even if he didn't know how to play the pipes.

It all turned out very well, after all. The daughter of the house married one of the sons of the MacNairs and changed her name back to Janet, her husband liking it better. And she had a "Mac" at the front of her name at last, as well as her share of the three MacNair bogles, so she was perfectly happy.

The mother and father grew a bit deaf with age, and the piping didn't trouble them at all.

But Tammas decided he'd had all he wanted of bogles and of St Andrews as well. So he went off to London where he made his fortune and became a real Sassenach. In time, he even got a "Sir" before his name, which gave him a lot more pleasure than he'd ever have got from a "Mac".

The bogle never did learn to play the bagpipes, though he never left off trying. But nobody cared about that at all. Not even the bogle.

Me and My Shadow

Eric Frank Russell

Little Trimble lowered a shaking apron, blinked his weak apologetic eyes.

'Now, now, Martha! Don't be like that!' he quavered.

Resting a beefy arm athwart her end of the breakfast table, Martha spoke slowly and viciously. Her voice was harsh with emotion, her features red with wrath, her expression venomous.

'For fifteen years I've lectured you, instructed you, commanded you. For seven hundred and eighty weeks of seven days each I've tried to do my duty as a wife by knocking some spark of manhood into your miserable body.' She slammed a huge, horny hand upon the table, made the milk jump in its jug. 'And what've I got?'

'Aw, Martha!'

'What I've got,' she bellowed, 'is exactly what I had right at the start – a crawling, quivering, undersized, cowardly, spineless and gutless little worm!'

'I ain't as bad as that,' he protested feebly.

'Prove it!' she shouted. 'Prove it! Go and do what

you haven't found the nerve to do in fifteen shiver-
ing years. Go and tell that boss of yours you've got
to have a raise.'

'*Tell* him?' Trimble blinked at her, aghast. 'You
mean *ask* him?'

'I said to *tell* him.' Her voice was bitingly sarcas-
tic, and still loud.

'He'll fire me.'

'Of course, you would think of that!' Down came
the hand again. The milk went over the top with
fixed bayonets, flopped, made a spatter in No Man's
Land. '*Let* him fire you. It'll be your chance. Tell
him you've waited for it fifteen years, then hand him
a poke in the gizzard. Find another job.'

'What if there *ain't* another job?' he asked, almost
tearfully.

'There's plenty. Dozens of them.' She stood up,
her mighty bulk still awing him despite years of
familiarity. 'Unfortunately, they're for men!'

He flinched, reached for his hat.

'I'll see,' he murmured.

'You'll see! You were going to see a year back.
And the year before that.'

Her voice followed him out the front door and a
hundred yards down the street. 'And the year before
that, and the one before that. Pfah!'

He mirrored himself in a window farther down.
There he was, well under average height, paunchy,
flabby, insignificant. Guess everybody was pretty
well right about him. Just a fat little slob.

A downtown bus came along. He reached the
door, got boosted in by a brawny hustler behind.
The hustler rough-housed past him while he stood
dumbly tendering the driver a quarter.

Trimble didn't say anything when a hard, heavy
elbow dented the flabbiness over his ribs. He was

quite used to it.

The driver slapped five nickels into his hand, scowled, shoved his machine in gear. Dropping a coin into the box, Trimble wandered to the back.

There was a vacant seat blocked by a blue-jowled individual. The sitter undressed Trimble with one contemptuous rip of his eyes, made no attempt to move.

Stretching himself, Trimble inserted pudgy fingers in a swinging handle, hung on without remark.

Dismounting ten blocks down, he crossed the road, his path including a deep safety curve around the backside of a policeman's horse. Trotting along the sidewalk, he reached the office.

Watson was already in. Trimble said, 'Good morning!' and Watson growled, 'Humph!' Every day their exchange was the same – good morning, and humph.

The others came in later. One replied to Trimble's greeting with what might have been, 'Marn!' or 'Garn!' The rest grunted, snorted, or grinned as if at a secret joke.

At ten, the boss made his advent. He never just turned up, or arrived, or landed. He always made an advent. This time was the same. The boss entered with the air of one about to lay a foundation-stone, or launch a battleship, or something. Nobody greeted him. They tried to look extremely respectful and very busy at one and the same time. Except Trimble, who managed to depict servile idleness.

He gave the boss an hour to get through the morning mail, then prayed for strength, knocked, went in.

'Excuse me, sir.'

'Hey?' The bison head came up, savage eyes transfixed the petitioner. 'Well, what d'you want?

'Nothing, sir, nothing,' assured Trimble, his blood turning to water. 'It wasn't important, and I've forgotten it.'

'Then get out!'

Trimble got out. Twelve o'clock came, and he tried to steel himself once more. There seemed to be a shortage of steel. He sat down again wearily.

At ten minutes to one, he tried for the third time, stood outside the boss's door, lifted his knuckles, and then changed his mind. He'd leave it until after lunch. The food would fortify him.

There was a bar on the way to the cafeteria. He'd passed it a thousand times, but had never gone inside. This time, it struck him that a shot of whisky might help. He'd heard it called Dutch courage, and any sort of courage – Dutch or Zulu – was something he could do with plenty.

Warily, his gaze went up and down the street. If Martha caught him in this sink of iniquity she'd fell him in his tracks. Yes, another Indian would bite the dust. But there wasn't any Martha. Greatly daring, he entered the bar.

The clients, or inmates, or whatever they're called, stared at him with open suspicion. Six of them were propped against the lengthy counter, their eyes summing him up as a barley-water addict. He'd have gone back if it hadn't been too late.

A bartender came along, said curtly, 'What's yours?'

'A drink.'

Somebody's snicker brought home to Trimble that one couldn't very well ask for a drink. One had to be more specific. For the life of him, he couldn't think of anything but beer. He didn't want beer.

'What's good?' he asked brightly.

'It depends.'

'Depends on what?'

'Whether you've got a thirst, a yen, or a woe!'

'I have,' said Trimble fervently, 'got a woe!'

'Leave it to me.' With an assured flick of his cloth the bartender went away. He did things with bottles, came back, placed before the customer a glass of cloudy, yellow liquid. 'That'll be forty.'

Trimble paid, sat and stared at the glass. It fascinated him. It frightened him. It was as full of invitation and terror as an uncoiled cobra. He was still looking at it five minutes later when his neighbour, a hefty six-footer, casually put out a hairy hand, took the glass, drained it at a gulp. On no one but Trimble could such a breach of saloon etiquette be perpetrated.

'Always glad to help a pal,' jeered the speaker's mouth, while his eyes said, 'Well, d'ya want to make anything out of it?'

Offering no retort, no protest, Trimble went out. The contempt on the bartender's face was a hurtful thing. The others' raucous laughter was a dancing flame that scorched his neck and ears.

Safely outside, he communed with himself. What was the matter with him that he should be at the receiving end of all the kicks and butts? Could he help it that he was not a rip-roaring tough? Wasn't it the way he was made? Most important of all, what could he do about it – if anything?

There were these something-analysts to whom one could appeal. But they were doctors of a sort. He was terrified of doctors with their background of hospitals and operations. Besides, he feared appealing to anyone lest his reward be ridicule. He'd had plenty of ridicule ever since he was a kid. Was there a thing he didn't fear – just one, single thing of which he wasn't scared?

Somebody spoke close by him.

'Now don't be frightened. Maybe I can help you.'

Turning, Trimble saw a little, white-haired man with a shrivelled form topped by a parchment face from which peered eyes of the clearest blue. The clothes this man wore were old-fashioned, curious, but his general appearance served to strengthen his expression of amiable understanding.

'I saw what happened in there.' The little man nodded towards the bar. 'I appreciate your position.'

'Why should it interest you?' asked Trimble guardedly.

'I'm always interested in people.' His friendly hand took Trimble's arm and they walked along side by side. 'People are infinitely more interesting than things.' The blue eyes twinkled gently. 'It is an iron rule that everybody has one outstanding fault, or, if you prefer, one fundamental weakness. The commonest one is fear. The man who fears no man may yet fear cancer. The dictator fears hidden thoughts. Many people fear death, and those who don't, fear life.'

'True,' conceded Trimble, thawing in spite of himself.

'You are a slave of fear,' went on the ancient. 'Your case is made malignant by your own consciousness of it. You are too aware.'

'Don't I know it!'

'That's exactly what I'm telling you! You know it. And it is always with you. You cannot forget it.'

'I wish I could,' said Trimble. 'Maybe someday I shall. Maybe I'll get guts. Heaven knows I've tried!'

'I'm sure you have.' The wizened one smiled happily. 'All a trier needs is the support of an ever-present friend. He craves encouragement, and, if need be, assistance. Every man has a friend of his own.'

'Show me mine,' challenged Trimble lugubriously. 'I'm a hell of a pal to myself.'

'You shall have the support gained only by a favoured few,' promised the other.

He looked around very cautiously, then felt in the depths of a pocket.

'You shall quaff from a fountain in nethermost Tibet.'

He produced a long, thin vial filled with liquid of iridescent green.

'This,' he whispered, 'will give you ears to hear the voice of darkness, a tongue to talk in tones of a ghost.'

'It'll *what*?'

'Take it,' urged the other. 'I give it because it is the law of Shan that grace shall beget grace, and strength shall father strength.' Another gentle smile. 'You have now only one fear to conquer – the fear to drink!'

He was gone. How he went was a mystery to the astonished Trimble. First, the little man was there, the next instant his wraithlike form had merged with distant pedestrians. Trimble stood, stared up the street, then at the vial clenched in plump fingers. He put the thing in his pocket.

Ten minutes to spare outside the time required to get back to the office. Trimble exited from the cafeteria, his stomach only half filled, his soul troubled. The choice lay between a scene with the boss or a scene with Martha. He was between the devil and the deep blue sea and the fact had spoiled his appetite.

Detouring around the block, he found a vacant lot free from scurrying people. Seeking the comparative privacy of the space's farthest corner, he took out the shining vial, had another look at it.

The contents were brilliantly green and looked oily. The stuff might be a drug, or even poison. If a drug could make gangsters hold up banks, what could it make him do? Or, if it was a poison, would it make him die peacefully and without pain? Would Martha weep when she saw him lying stiff and cold, a saintlike expression upon his waxen face?

Uncapping the vial, he put his nose to it, got a whiff of dreamy elusive odours. He stuck in the tip of his tongue, licked it around his mouth, absorbing the flavour. Strong, aromatic, enticing. Putting the vial to his lips, he swigged the contents to the last drop. It was the first chance he had ever taken, the most reckless thing he had ever done.

'And about time, too!' commented an eerie voice.

Trimble looked around. There wasn't anybody near him. He threw away the empty vial, decided he'd been deluded.

'Down here,' hinted the voice.

'Uhm?' Trimble stared in a circle. Nobody! Gosh, that must have been a potent brew – he was imagining things already.

'Down here,' urged the voice with sudden impatience. 'On the floor, you barrel-shaped lump of stupidity!' A pause, then complainingly: 'I'm your shadow.'

'Oh, suffering snakes!' mouthed Trimble, covering his face with quivering hands. 'I'm talking to my shadow! I've got the rats on one drink!'

'Don't be such a damned dope!' reproved the shadow. 'Every man's got his black ghost, but not every guy can use or understand shady language.' Silence, while the shade pondered, then the blunt command: 'Come on – we're going places.'

'Where?'

'We're going to beat up that man in the bar.'

'What?' yelled Trimble, at the top of his voice. A couple of pedestrians stopped dead on the sidewalk, gaped across the lot. Trimble took no notice. His mind was a whirl of wild confusion, his whole being tormented by fear of the strait-jacket and the padded cell.

'Don't be so all-fired noisy.'

The ghost faded slightly as a cloud crossed the sun, then came back at full strength. 'Now that we can pow-wow, I reckon I'd better have a name. You can call me Clarence.'

'Cl . . . Cl . . . Cl . . .'

'Sure! Anything wrong with it?', demanded the other aggressively. 'Shut up! Get over here, nearer the wall – that's right! See me sitting up? See me big – bigger'n you? Now bend that right arm. Okay, take a look at mine. A humdinger, huh? What wouldn't Dempsey give for a limb like this!'

'God!' groaned Trimble pitifully, his arm bent, his eyes turned appealing to the sky.

'You'n me,' went on Clarence, 'can now co-operate. You do the aiming, and I'll hand the wallops. You've got to make sure you get the right side of the light to make me big and strong, then we'll lash out together. Just take good aim, remembering that I'm with you. Every time you hand a guy a prod, I'll paste him one that'll hang him on a ledge twelve floors up. D'you understand?'

'Y-yes,' admitted Trimble, his voice almost inaudible. He cast a leery glance at his rear, saw that the number of onlookers had increased to ten.

'Turn around so's I'll be behind you,' ordered the shadow. 'Take a swipe by yourself, then another one with me. You'll be surprised at the difference.'

Obediently, Trimble turned, faced the grinning audience, plunged his pudgy fist into thin air. It was a futile effort, and he knew it. Drawing back, he swung again, using all his strength and weight. His arm shot out like a piston, dragging his body off balance. He stumbled forward. The spectators laughed.

'See? What did I tell you? Not one guy in ten knows his own strength.' Clarence permitted himself a ghostly chuckle. 'Now we're all set. How about laying those kibitzers in a row, just to get our hand in?'

'No!' shouted Trimble. He wiped perspiration from a crimson half-crazed face. The audience went up to fifteen.

'Okay, have it your own way. Now let's get back to the bar, and remember, I'm always with you!'

With his feet dragging more and more reluctantly, Trimble reached the bar. He stood outside, knees knocking, while his bellicose shade gave quick instructions.

'Nobody can hear me but you. You're one of the favoured few who can hear and speak the language of the dark. We'll go in there together, and you'll do what I tell you to do, say what I tell you to say. Whatever happens, don't get scared – I'll be with you, and I could flop a bull elephant.'

'You b-bet,' agreed Trimble with total lack of enthusiasm.

'All right. What are you waiting for?'

Like a condemned criminal pacing the thirteen fateful steps, Trimble moved through the doors and into the bar. The same gang was still there, the same beefy hijacker lounging at the nearer end.

The bartender took one look at the entrant, smirked, then jerked an informative thumb. The hijacker sat pat and scowled. Still smirking, the bar-tender came up.

'What can I do for you?'

'Switch on the lights,' gasped Trimble in an un-earthly voice, 'and I'll show you something.'

Now he'd done it! He'd committed himself be-yond withdrawal. He'd have to go through with the whole whacky affair right until the interns came and bore him away.

The bartender considered. Whatever was going to be shown, it could be twisted into something that would add to the day's fun. He decided to oblige.

'Sure!' he said, and switched them on.

Trimble looked around, absorbed a sudden dose of confidence. It was the sight at his side. There was Clarence towering up the wall like a mighty dijnn.

'Go on,' commanded the tremendous shadow. 'Do your stuff!'

Taking one step forward, Trimble snatched up the hijacker's glass, flung its contents into the fellow's face.

The recipient arose like one in a dream, gasped, mopped his streaming features, gasped again. Then he removed his jacket, folded it carefully, placed it on the counter. He spoke to his opponent very slowly, very deliberately, and very politely.

'I ain't rolling in money, but my heart is bursting with charity. I'll see that you get a decent burial!' With that, he released a pile-driver.

'Duck!' yelped Clarence.

Trimble pulled his head into his boots, felt an express locomotive rush across his hair.

'Now!' screamed Clarence frantically.

Popping up, Trimble slammed out a fist, concentrat-ing on his aim, but putting all his weight and strength behind the blow. He tried for the Adam's apple, got it, and for a moment thought he was going to stick his arm through the man's neck. It was something like walloping the sixtieth floor of the Empire State Building, and the effect was just as spectacular. The fellow went down like a poled ox. Oh boy, had he got power.

'Again!' raved Clarence. 'Lemme soak him another as he gets up.'

The smitten one was struggling to rise, an expression of absolute incredulity upon his face. He got halfway, making uncertain motions with his arms and legs.

Trimble wound up his right arm until he could almost hear it whiz. Then he let his fist fly, this time trying for the other's smeller. He got it with a loud swack like the sound of a skied baseball. The victim tried to throw his head clean off his shoulders, then collapsed and slid a foot along the floor.

'G-g-gosh!' stuttered an awed voice.

Shaking with excitement, Trimble turned his back on his supine opponent, went to the counter. The bartender came up, his features wearing an expression of deep respect. Trimble licked his own forefinger, drew a spit face inside a beer-ring on the counter.

'Put curls on that!'

The bartender hesitated, looked around with a beseeching air, swallowed hard. Meekly, he licked his finger, added the curls.

Reaching over, Trimble snatched the fellow's cloth.

'This is what'll happen next time you pull faces at me.' He rubbed out the face.

'Now, Mister, don't get tough,' pleaded the bartender.

'Nuts!' It was the first time Trimble had used the

word as a retort. He shied the cloth back, had a look at his snoring victim, walked out.

As his plump little form passed through the doors, a customer said, 'That guy sure is dynamite!·Looks to me like he's full of dope, and ripe for a killing.'

'I dunno.' The bartender was both subdued and sheepish. 'You can't never tell from the looks of them. Take Slugs McKeefe, he's a world-beater at his weight, but he's only a fat little guy. I didn't like that feller's looks from the first – he might be Slug's brother.'

'He might,' conceded the critic thoughtfully.

Down on the floor, the stricken one's bubbling snore ended in a gasp, a gulp, and an oath. He stirred, tried to sit up.

Out on the street, Clarence said, delight in his voice, 'Now for the boss.'

'No, no, not that!' Trimble's apologetic face was crimson from the strain of his recent adventure. His eyes kept flickering back, searching for the murderous pursuit that he thought was inevitable. It was hard to believe that he'd actually done what he had done, and he couldn't understand how he'd escaped alive.

'I said now for the boss, you animated pumpkin!' repeated the shadow, with much asperity.

'But I daren't batter the boss.' Trimble's voice grew to a loud protesting wail. 'It'll get me in stir.'

'*What'll* get you in stir?' demanded a passer-by, stopping and staring at the distracted speaker.

'Nothing – I was talking to myself.' Trimble stopped as his irritated shadow snarled an interruption. He was reluctant to take the offered advice, but it looked as if he had to. 'Hey!' he called. His questioner came back.

'Mind your own damn' business,' said Trimble rudely.

'Okay, okay, keep your hair on!' The other was startled, hurried away.

'See?' chortled Clarence. 'Now for the boss. We won't get hard unless we hafta.'

'Have to,' corrected Trimble.

'Hafta,' Clarence persisted. 'We'll talk first. If he won't appease us, we'll resort to force.' He was quiet for a moment, then added: 'And don't forget the lights – I like to grow powerful before I slap 'em.'

'Oh, all right.' Trimble began to feel resigned to a course of events that eventually was going to dump him in a cell, if not in the morgue. With a sigh of martyrdom, he entered the building, went upstairs to the office.

'Afternoon!'

'Humph!' said Watson.

Switching on the office lights, Trimble looked around, located his shady partner, then walked up close to Watson, and spoke in a very loud voice.

'I don't expect anything but a grunt from a pig. Might I remind you that I bade you good afternoon?'

'Eh? . . . ah! . . . huh?' Watson was both scared and thunderstruck. 'Ah! . . . very well . . . good afternoon!'

'That's right! Remember it in future.' With numb feet and a whirling brain, Trimble went across to the boss's door. He raised his knuckles to knock.

'Don't!' swore Clarence.

Trimble shuddered, grasped the door-knob, turned it gently. Taking a deep breath, he gave the door a tremendous thrust that sent it back with a crash. The thing almost flew off its hinges. As the boss shot up from behind his desk, Trimble walked in.

'You,' roared the boss, vibrating with rage, 'you're fired!'

Turning, Trimble went back, closing the maltreated door behind him. He didn't say a word.

'Trimble,' bellowed the boss, his voice reverberating behind the door, 'come here.'

Trimble entered for the second time. Closing the door on extended ears in the outer office, he scowled at the boss, then went to the wall, switched on the lights. After that, he fooled around until he got a position that made Clarence ceiling-high. The boss squatted and watched all this, his face purple, his eyes popping.

They stared at each other awhile, their silence broken only by the boss's heavy asthmatic breathing. Finally, the latter spoke.

'Have you been drinking, Trimble?'

'My taste in liquid refreshment is not a matter for discussion,' said Trimble, flatly. 'I came in to tell you that I've resigned.'

Stark horror filled his soul as the fateful words fell from his lips. He'd done it now! Which was worse, Clarence or Martha? He didn't know – but he sure had burned his boats.

'Resigned?' parroted the boss, mouthing it as if it was some new, outlandish word.

'Sure! I'm fed up. I'm going to offer my services to Rubinstein and Flanagan.' The boss shied like a frightened horse, and he went desperately on: 'They'll pay me well for what I know. I'm sick and tired of my lousy salary.'

'Now Trimble,' said the boss, gasping for breath. 'I've no desire to part with you after your many years of service. I would not like to see your undoubted talents wasted on a gang of pikers like Rubinstein and Flanagan. I'll give you another two dollars a week.'

'Lemme wipe his face off his neck,' suggested Clarence, eagerly.

'No!' shouted Trimble.

'Three dollars,' said the boss.

'Come on – just one crack,' Clarence persisted.

'No!' yelled Trimble, sweating at every pore.

'All right, I'll give you five.' The boss's face contorted. 'And that's final.'

Mopping his brow, Trimble felt as if he was nearing the end of an hour upon the rack. Perspiration trickled down his spine, and his legs felt weak.

'I've been grossly underpaid the last ten years, and I wouldn't stay with you for a raise of less than twelve bucks. I'm worth an extra twenty to you, but I'm willing to take twelve, and let you have eight for cigars.'

'C-c-cigars!'

'Rubinstein and Flanagan'll raise me twelve. You can do it – or do without.'

'Twelve!' The boss was dumbfounded, then annoyed, then thoughtful. Eventually, he reached a decision.

'It seems, Trimble, that I have been guilty of underestimating your abilities. I'll give you the increase for which you ask' – he bent forward and glared – 'in exchange for a fidelity bond.'

'Okay. I'll stay.' Making for the door, he opened it, said, 'Thanks!'

'See?' said Clarence.

Without answering his nagging shade, Trimble took his seat at his desk.

In tones audible all over the room, he spoke to Watson.

'Nice weather we're having.'

'Humph!'

'EH?' Trimble bawled.

'Very nice,' replied Watson, meekly . . . .

His heart sang like a nest of nightingales while he worked through the afternoon. Somehow, the story of his affair with the boss leaked around the office. People spoke to him in manner different from that of yore. It was almost incredible, but he was getting something he'd never had before – respect.

Rain was hammering down when he closed his books and left for home. What did it matter? The stinging drops felt good on his plump, beaming face, and the air was like old wine. Disdaining the bus, he walked along the wet, shining avenue, whistling to himself as he trotted along. He'd got news that would paralyse Martha!

A noise came from around the next corner, an explosive sound like that of a burst tyre. Then another and another and another. Running feet pounded somewhere around the angle of the corner building. He came level, saw two figures racing toward him. One was six jumps behind the other, and both had guns. The nearest of the sprinting pair was twenty yards away. It was his opponent in the bar!

Spears of fear jabbed themselves into Trimble's brain. There was an uproar further down the street, and it looked like the running pair were making a frantic getaway. If the leader recognised Trimble, he'd seize the chance to blot him out in full flight. There was nowhere to hide in those split-seconds, no place in which to bury himself until the danger had passed. Even worse, the sky was heavily clouded, and his precious shadow was gone.

'Clarence!' he screamed, fearfully.

No reply. His shout drew the leading fugitive's attention. The fellow knew him immediately, sucked back thin lips in a deathly grin, raised his weapon. He was almost upon his quaking victim, the range was less than one yard, and it was impossible to miss.

Trimble kicked him on the knee-cap.

He didn't do it on the impulse of the moment, nor with the desperation of a cornered rat. He was driven to it by the inevitable conclusion that his only hope lay in behaving exactly as if his missing shadow was still in support. So he lashed out with his foot, striving to connect accurately, using every ounce of his strength.

The other promptly plunged on to his face as if determined to poke his head through the sidewalk and have a look at the subway. It was a heartening sight that made Trimble suspect his efficient shade might still be hanging around even though unseen. The thought lent him courage.

With the startled expression of one who has seen an ant miraculously change into a lion, the second runner pulled up almost chest to chest with Trimble. He was a tall, lanky specimen whose Adam's apple seemed beyond reach.

Trimble batted his stomach against his spine. The fellow gagged, bent his upper half to a convenient angle, and Trimble bashed the apple. The victim did not assume the expected horizontal position. His sallow features suffused with a mixture of hatred and agony, he straightened, swiped at Trimble with the barrel of his weapon.

The blow failed to connect. Following former practice, Trimble sucked his head into his shoulders, blew it up again, stabbed another one into the stomach. The face came down once more and he smacked it up with considerable vim.

A crash sounded behind him, and a red-hot wasp bit off the lobe of his left ear. He took no notice, and

he concentrated upon the face to the complete ex-
clusion of everything else. Foul oaths were pouring
from somewhere near the source of the crash, heavy
feet were thumping the sidewalk towards him,
people were shouting and whooping all around.

He heard none of it. His mind had no knowledge
of his first assailant's resurrection. That snarling pan
opposite his own was his sole object in life, the one
purpose of his being.

With aim and weight and strength, he bashed the
face up, socked it down, clouted it backward. Something hard and knobbly exploded out of nothingness, seemed to tear the left cheekbone from his own
head. Another one appeared to tear his ribs apart.
But Trimble kept working on that face, battering it
into a bloody mask and pounding in the gore.

His heart was a jitterbug, and his breath coming in
whistling sobs when a long, black object sailed over
the hateful face, descended, pushing it down to the
floor. He made a couple more automatic swiping
motions, then stood shuddering and blinking. His
vision cleared slowly.

The cop said, 'Mister, for a feller your size you
sure are sudden death!'

Looking around, Trimble saw that half a dozen
cops had arrived, and were bundling up his recent
opponents.

'That first guy,' went on the other, 'was Ham
Carlotti, and we've wanted him for months.' He
clothed Trimble in admiration. 'We owe you one for
this. Any time we can do something for you, just
ask.'

Getting out a handkerchief, Trimble dabbed his
ear, looked at the handkerchief. There was blood on
it. Wow! He was bleeding like a stuck pig! And his
left eye was swelling up, his cheekbone felt like hell,

his ribs were a torment. He was in a devil of a mess!

'You can do something for me right now,' he told the cop. 'Ever since I was a kid I've wanted to ride home in a police car. How about it?'

'You bet!' the cop enthused. 'It'll be a pleasure.' He called to the driver of a car that had just swung in. 'This gent's been a help. The ride's on us.'

'Where d'ya live?'

Clambering in, Trimble sat back and enjoyed himself. Off they went, hell-for-leather, the siren yelling like a banshee, traffic scuttling madly from their path. This was the life!

The sun came out, beaming at full strength. He became aware of his shadow riding by his side.

'Clarence.'

'Yes, Master,' he said very humbly.

'In future, you can leave it to me.'

'Yes, Master. But . . .'

'Shut up!' bawled Trimble.

'Shut up who?' inquired the driver, glancing surprisedly over his shoulder.

'The missus,' Trimble answered glibly. 'I'm ready for war.'

Smiling broadly, the driver whirled his car into the curb, followed his passenger to the door. When Martha opened it, he touched his cap, said: 'Ma'am, your husband's a hero.' Then he went.

'Hero!' snorted Martha. Crossing brawny arms on her ample bosom, she braced herself for an informative speech. Then her eyes found her partner's war-scarred face. She let the eyes protrude. 'Where've you been, to get a mug like that?'

Vouchsafing no reply, Trimble pushed past her, went into the hall. He waited until she had closed the door, then put skinned knuckles on his hips, faced her squarely. He had a kindly nature, and he had no desire to hurt her unduly, but it was now necessary to impress this woman that she had to deal with a man.

'Martha, I've slapped down a couple of gangsters, and I've soaked the boss another twelve bucks.' He blinked as she clutched at the wall for support. He drew a deep breath. 'I've been very patient with you for many years, but I've reached the end of my tether, and from now on I want no more of your lip.'

'Lip?' she echoed dazedly, not believing her ears.

'Otherwise, I'll paste you one that'll make you wish you'd brought your parachute.'

'Horatio!' She staggered forward, her face a picture of utter stupefaction. 'You wouldn't strike a *woman* would you?'

'Wouldn't I!' He spat on his sore knuckles.

'Oh, Horatio!' In one wild swoop she had embraced his neck and found his protesting lips.

Heck, aren't women peculiar critters? They liked 'em gentle, but a few – like Martha – preferred 'em tough. Might as well give her more of the same.

Grabbing her hair, he pulled her face over to a comfortable slant. Then he kissed her. He concentrated on aim, weight, and strength. It was a pouting, juicy, emphatic osculation that finished in a loud report.

Grinning triumphantly, he peeked over her shoulder to see what his subdued shadow thought of that. But Clarence was too busy to bother. Didn't Martha have a shadow too?

The Gargoyle

Roger Malisson

Miss Harper, the science teacher, said it sounded like a herd of mad elephants; but Mr Groves, who took games, said it was more like a flock of parrots.

'It' was the noise made by Forms 1A and 1B milling round the bus which was to take them on their annual history outing. Fifty-eight boys and girls were boarding it together, though as the driver kept roaring out, the doorway wouldn't take them all at once.

'One at a time, you perishing little – one at a time!' he appealed over and over again, and was ignored. Finally Mr Morris the history teacher appeared and quelled the riot with a thundering threat to send home *instantly* anyone who misbehaved.

'They can't do that,' muttered Beverley Riley to her best friend Christine Lee. 'My dad's already paid. I'm not getting off even if they tell me to.'

She was huddled with Christine on the best seat at the very back of the bus. It had been only the work of a moment to persuade the previous occupant to leave, by the simple but effective method of threatening to strike him over the head with Christine's vacuum flask.

'I'm glad we're going on holiday,' said Christine, settling back.

'It's only a rotten day trip to an old church!' said Beverley contemptuously. 'Anybody'd think you were going to rotten Spain!'

Christine did not answer because just then the driver started the engine and a cheer went up that drowned everything, even Philip Smith's frantic cry that he had left his packed lunch behind. Once through the school gates, the bus headed noisily and swiftly for the motorway. The history outing to Church Milton had begun.

'We might go past our house,' said Christine wistfully. 'I might see Mum and Gran and Kevin.' She peered hopefully out of the window, a quiet, timid, short-sighted little girl with pale fluffy hair and a vaguely pretty face.

Beside her Beverley Riley gave a snort of disgust. She was bigger, tougher, and cleverer than her friend. 'Your house isn't this way, silly! Anyway your Mum's at work and Kevin's in the nursery – here, have a crisp.' She thrust the bag under Christine's nose, and when Christine took one, made her take a whole handful. Beverley Riley was rough, but very generous.

'Mum's not at work,' said Christine plaintively. 'She's working nights, Beverley, Mum's not—'

'Oh, shut up!' snapped Beverley irritably. '*I* don't care where your rotten Mum is do I?' There was a noisy minute or two while Christine objected to her mother being called 'rotten', and then for a while peace reigned as each girl swore never to speak to the other again.

'Anyway,' said Beverley finally, screwing up her

crisp bag and throwing it under the seat, 'Anyway I'm glad I'm not speaking to you, Christine Lee, because you're soft, and when I do my magic charm you'd only run off and tell somebody.'

'What magic charm?' asked Christine at once, forgetting she had just vowed she would never have anything to do with Beverley in her life again, ever. 'What magic charm, Bev?'

'I'm not telling you,' said Beverley stubbornly.

It took Christine almost ten minutes to make her change her mind.

'Well,' whispered Beverley at last, 'I went to the library, see, and I found a book all about this church we're going to.'

'A book!' muttered Christine, impressed. She was a very poor reader herself and never deliberately went looking for books.

'And it had a picture of the church and a gargoyle up on the roof —'

'A gargle?' Christine broke in, mystified. 'What gargle?'

Beverley went into fits of laughter and finally explained to her friend that a 'gargoyle' was the name for an ugly kind of statue they sometimes had on the roofs of old churches.

'Anyway this church has got one as well, and it's a really horrible one, and if you say the magic charm over it – *it comes alive!*'

'Ugh, no,' said Christine, shutting her eyes in delicious terror.

'Yes,' said Beverley, and suddenly hooked her fingers like claws and made a hideous face, moaning, 'I'm coming, I'm coming, to get YOU!!'

Christine let out a scream that nearly made the driver run into the lorry in front. After that Mr Morris made them sit apart for the rest of the journey.

Church Milton was a village, very small compared to the big industrial town Beverley and Christine came from. Hundreds of years ago it had been quite an important place and a handsome church had been built there which still stood, on the sloping ground above the main street. A neat graveyard was spread around it, and a lych gate stood at the front of the path which led to the arched main door.

'Isn't it lovely?' said Christine as she climbed out of the coach.

'Stop here a moment all of you,' said Mr Morris as the classes swarmed around him. Oddly enough the fact that they were in the country and away from the noisy traffic had calmed all of them down. They still larked about, but without yelling very much.

'Does anybody know why this is called a "lych gate"?' asked Mr Morris, staring at them all in turn.

'Yeah,' said Beverley loudly. 'It's because they used to put dead bodies under it before they were taken in to be buried, and "lych" means body, sir.' She basked in the silent admiration of the class.

'Quite right Beverley,' said Mr Morris approvingly. 'Does anyone know anything about the church?'

'Please sir, it's got a gargle on the roof!' Christine burst out, then yelped in pain as Beverley trod on her foot.

'That's right, very good, Christine,' said Mr Morris in surprise. 'Mind what you're doing, Beverley. Now, look up on the roof all of you —' he pointed, and fifty-eight children stared upwards. 'Can you see that dark, hunched shape up there? That is a gargoyle. Now a gargoyle,' he continued impressively, 'is a grotesque statue sometimes carved over the waterspouts of medieval churches. "Grotesque" means misshapen and ugly – very similar to the face you're pulling now, Smith.' Everyone laughed and Philip Smith stopped trying to amuse his friends by exaggerated squinting. 'This gargoyle has a legend attached to it,' Mr Morris went on slowly. 'According to the old story, a witch who lived here in the village hundreds of years ago had the power of casting a spell on it, which would make it come to life during the hours of darkness. Then it would do whatever the witch told it, including breaking into houses and carrying off her enemies. Nobody could stop it because it was tremendously strong, and arrows and swords just bounced off its stone skin. In the morning the witch's enemies would be found dead at the bottom of the church tower, all their bones broken.'

When he had finished there was a satisfactory, fascinated silence.

'Of course, it's only a story. Right.' Mr Morris glanced at his watch. 'All of you are to be back here for three o'clock. Don't drop litter, don't trespass in people's gardens and don't go outside the village. Clear? Off you go, then.'

They trooped away reasonably quietly. Beverley and Christine waited behind until the others had gone.

'Now then, where's my charm.' Beverley began to rummage through her bag.

'Oh, don't bother about it, Bev.' Christine dithered uncertainly. It wasn't that she really believed Beverley's charm would work, she just didn't want to see it tried.

'Where've I put it? Where's the rotten thing gone? I know I put it – ah!' Beverley waved a scrap of paper in triumph. 'See, it's here. Right then, come on!' She ran off impatiently through the lych gate and up the gravel path to the church, with Christine following reluctantly.

Inside the church it was cool and shady. Dust floated slowly in the broad sunbeams that shone through the plain glass windows. They tiptoed to the back of the church and through a door marked 'PRIVATE', which led to a narrow stone room with a flight of curving steps at the end. It was the entrance to the church tower.

'It's up here,' whispered Beverley, and clutched Christine's arm. 'Come on!' Quickly the two girls began to climb.

Their legs were aching by the time they reached the top of the stairs. The day had clouded over and as they came up on to the tower roof, which was flat and encircled by a parapet, a breeze sprang up that made Christine shiver. She refused to go near the wall to look at the dizzying view, but Beverley lived on the fourteenth floor of a block of flats and heights did not bother her. Suddenly she gave a little yelp of joy and beckoned her friend over.

'It's here! Chris, come and look!'

Cautiously Christine crept forward and peeped over the edge of the parapet, while Beverley craned over, dangerously far.

The statue was crouched at one corner of the tower, squatting on a stone ledge. It was about four feet high and shaped something like a man, but a dwarfish, muscular man with bulging eyes and a protruding tongue. Two bat-like wings spread up from its heavy shoulders. Its chin was resting on its clawed hand as if it were deep in thought.

'It looks like my Dad when he's doing the Pools,' giggled Beverley irreverently.

'Come away from the wall, Beverley,' said Christine in alarm. 'You'll fall.'

Beverley unfolded the paper with the charm written on it. She grinned, and began to chant in an eerie voice. Christine turned pale.

'Fetter, fetter, stane and blood,
I bid thee work to do me good.
By salt and fi, by wet and dry,
Thou stane of power I bid thee hie.'

'It's wicked to do magic in a church! I'm going!'
fretted Christine. Beverley waved her arms, swaying
from side to side for dramatic effect.

'My eyes to thine eyes,
My heart to thy breast,
Cast off thy sleep
And break thy rest.
To free thee from the gripe of stanes,
I give my blood unto thy veins – oh help!'

Christine gave a shriek and darted forward to
catch her friend as Beverley stumbled on the uneven
flagstones beneath their feet and knocked her chin
on the parapet.

'I bit my rotten tongue,' said Beverley indistinct-
ly. A trickle of blood ran down her chin. 'Have you
got a hanky?'

'It's gone on your collar,' said Christine dolefully,
dabbing the blood away.

'Never mind,' said Beverley, smearing her mouth
with the back of her hand. 'Did it work?'

They peered over the parapet. The gargoyle sat
hunched up below them, as disappointingly stony as
ever, staring out over the distant hills just as it had
done for the past six hundred years.

'Mr Morris said it was only a story,' said Christine,
heaving a sigh. 'Oh well. Come on, let's go.'

'Just a minute,' said Beverley. 'See that?' she

pointed to a dark splash that lay like a tear on the gargoyle's gritty cheek. 'That's blood, look, my blood.' She smiled proudly, then stiffened with excitement as her eyes roamed past the statue to the road below. 'Hey, there's an ice-cream van down there! Come on!'

The two girls ran like lightning for the door and within a moment the tower roof was empty and the gargoyle was left alone again to its silent vigil.

That night Christine's mother asked Mrs Riley if Beverley could stay overnight at their home. Mrs Lee was working part of a night shift at the local factory until midnight. Christine's grandmother, who lived with them, had been called away unexpectedly to visit a sick relative and her father was working in Scotland for a few weeks.

Beverley and Christine were delighted with the arrangement.

'Now don't start fooling about just because you're on your own tonight,' said Mrs Lee, tying on her headscarf. 'You've got the phone number of the factory, so ring me if anything happens. If Kevin wakes up you can bring him downstairs with you to watch television. Keep the fireguard up. There's tea in the flask so you won't have to boil the kettle or touch the oven, and there's orange juice in the fridge. Don't eat all the biscuits. Put the chain on the door when I go out and don't open up for anyone but me. Mrs Nelson next door is keeping an eye on you. If you aren't both in bed by the time I get home there'll be trouble. Give me a kiss now, there's a good girl. And remember, Beverley, no messing about.'

The front door eventually closed behind Mrs Lee.

'Goodbye Mum!' shouted Christine as the footsteps faded down the path, waving as if her mother could see her through the door. Beverley was already in the kitchen, opening the fridge.

They brought a tray loaded with orange juice, biscuits and cheese and sat nibbling in front of the fire, watching TV. During the first hour they went upstairs at ten-minute intervals to check that Kevin was still asleep in his cot. He was, though Christine suffered from fears that he had stopped breathing and kept creeping forward to listen. They went into Mrs Lee's bedroom to try on some of her dresses, then got ready for bed and came back downstairs to bank up the fire. It was while Beverley was lifting the scuttle to hurl coal on the fire that they heard a kind of rumbling noise outside.

'What's that?' Christine, terrified, clutched Beverley's nightgown.

The noise came again, heavy crunching thuds as if someone were trying to climb the coal pile beneath the kitchen window outside.

'A burglar! Is the back door locked?' hissed Beverley.

'Yes. Oh Mum. I'm scared,' whimpered Christine, ready to cry. Beverley did not feel very brave herself but she wanted to be sure it wasn't boys fooling around before they phoned Mrs Lee. After all, it was only half past eight; it was barely dark.

'I'm going to peep out of the back window,' she said.

Together they crept into the kitchen and Christine trembled while Beverley hauled herself up on to the draining board to peer cautiously into the dark back yard. At first she could see nothing, but as her eyes became used to the dusk she gradually made out the coal pile, the clothes line, Kevin's little car and two dustbins.

Two dustbins?

'Chris,' Beverley whispered, 'how many dustbins have you got?'

'One,' answered her friend in surprise.

Suddenly, what Beverley had taken for a second dustbin stirred at the sound of voices and shuffled awkwardly towards the window.

'Oh, no,' said Beverley in horror. 'Oh, *no*.'

'What is it? I'm fetching the police,' cried Christine, backing away.

'You can't call the police,' said Beverley. She turned round, her eyes big as saucers. 'Chris, it's the *gargoyle*.'

They stared at each other in panic, each thinking the same thing; whoever they called to help them would want to know what the gargoyle was doing there in the first place, and who had brought it . . . .

'I don't understand,' Beverley muttered. 'It didn't come alive at first. Why is it here now?'

Christine thought deeply for a moment and came up with the correct solution.

'It's gone dark,' she said. 'The spell only works while it's dark. That's why it didn't wake up before now.'

Outside the kitchen window the gargoyle shuffled impatiently.

'But what does it *want?*' cried Beverley. 'I didn't tell it to come here!' On impulse, she tried a command. 'Gargoyle! Go back!'

The gargoyle evidently took things literally. It began striding clumsily but firmly backwards, and if Beverley had not yelled 'Stop!' it would undoubtedly have smashed clean through the wall and into the alley. One thing was obvious, however; it would do anything she said. She jumped down from the draining board and began to unbolt the back door.

'Don't let it in!' yelped Christine. 'Tell it to go home!'

'I just tried that, didn't I?' snapped Beverley. 'It nearly knocked the wall down!'

'Perhaps you didn't say it right,' suggested Christine as Beverley opened the door. 'Try saying, "Gargoyle, go back to the church tower. In Church Milton. Cheshire",' she added as an afterthought.

'Gargoyle,' began Beverley in a quavering voice. Immediately the thing clumped forward and Beverley forgot to be brave and fled panic-stricken into the house with Christine almost trampling her down from behind. The stone monster followed them patiently, plodding across the kitchen lino and crushing the dog's food bowl into a shapeless lump.

The two frightened girls backed into a corner of the living-room. There was a crash as the gargoyle knocked a geranium off the hall table, then it appeared in the doorway. As it entered the light the girls had their first good look at it.

The gargoyle was still stone-skinned and even had bird droppings in its carved hair, but the face had changed. The tongue was drawn back into its mouth, and although it was still amazingly hideous it had a more normal appearance. It was even grinning slightly, as if it was enjoying its trip down from the tower after all those centuries of stillness. Its bulging eyes rolled slyly round the room until it caught sight of the girls huddled in the corner, and then it lumbered across the carpet towards them.

'Stop!' yelled Beverley desperately. The gargoyle halted with one foot planted in the middle of the tray which had been lying in front of the fire. A puddle of orange juice, biscuit crumbs and broken glass slowly formed on the rug. 'Oh, why don't you go home?' said Beverley. 'Can't you speak?'

The gargoyle grinned a huge banana grin and shook its ugly head.

'Maybe we could send it home on a bus,' suggested Christine hesitatingly.

'Oh sure,' snarled Beverley, exasperated. 'How would it get on a bus looking like that? The driver would have a fit!'

'If it went upstairs . . . ?' said Christine vaguely.

'. . . And came straight down through the floor. It must weigh half a ton. Try not to be an idiot, Christine!'

'Well, I'm not having it here when my Mum comes home!' gabbled Christine, beside herself. 'What'll she say when she sees it there on the carpet, you can't hoover round it or anything and our Kevin will cry or he might get trodden on when he's crawling about trying to play with it and – and . . . it'll have to go, Bev.'

'Well *I* can't get rid of it, can I?' Beverley stamped her foot in rage.

The two girls glared at each other, flushed, then slowly calmed down. Beverley was struck by a horrifying thought. What if the gargoyle stayed till morning, then *froze back?* How would they get it out of the house then? Mrs Lee would be furious. Christine too was having worrying thoughts.

'Do you think they'll miss it at the church?' she said doubtfully. 'Will they notice it's gone?'

'Of course they will!' shouted Beverley. 'How could anybody possibly not notice a four-foot-high gargoyle when it's not there?' The strain of it all was making her a trifle incoherent. 'You'd notice that ugly rotten thing anywhere!' In her annoyance she grabbed a hairbrush off the mantelpiece and threw it at the gargoyle's head. There was a snapping sound as the gargoyle suddenly shot out its long tongue

and swallowed the hairbrush at a gulp like a frog
catching a fly. Then it grinned appreciatively.

'That was nice, was it?' said Christine astonished.

Beverley thought hard. Where could they put the
thing? Where would a big ugly statue not be
noticed? She snapped her fingers as an idea came.

'I know!' she cried. 'We'll take it to Hannock
Park!'

Hannock Park was a few streets away. It already
had some life-sized statues of local politicians in it,
grim-faced men in top hats and old-fashioned
clothes; maybe nobody would notice an extra one.
Beverley did not care where the statue was found, as
long as it was not in Mrs Lee's front room.

'How will it get there?' asked Christine.

'It'll have to walk,' answered Beverley, and instantly she realised that the gargoyle could not go
through the streets dressed, or undressed, as it was,
without attracting attention. 'Chris – have you got
any old clothes?'

They finally dressed the gargoyle in Christine's
granny's old coat. It had a velvet collar and an ivory
brooch but apart from these unsuitable features it
served very well. On Beverley's command the gargoyle stuck its hands enthusiastically into the arm-
holes; there was a dreadful sound of lining tearing
and Christine winced.

They eyed the gargoyle as it stood on the hearth-
rug, still grinning, its hideous head poking up from
the velvet collar. The sleeves of the coat were so long
that they hid its hands completely, and the hem was
almost brushing the floor.

'We'd better see if it can walk in it,' muttered
Beverley. 'Walk about a bit, gargoyle.'

The gargoyle circled round the settee with a
curious hump-backed shuffle, like an old tramp

looking for dropped pennies.

'Stop. That's good,' said Beverley. The gargoyle nodded and flicked its tongue in and out of its mouth like a snake.

'Don't get carried away,' scolded Beverley.

'What about my Gran's rainhat?' suggested Christine, in a burst of inspiration. They fetched it and tied it over the gargoyle's carved curls. Christine was so pleased with the success of her idea that she brought an umbrella for it to hold.

Then they dashed upstairs and dressed hurriedly. Christine would not leave her little brother alone in the house so they wrapped him in blankets and put him in his pushchair, still sleeping. Making sure she had a key, Christine led the little procession out of the house and started up the street.

'Christine Lee! What do you think you're doing, taking Kevin out at this time of night? Where are you going?' They all froze in horror at the sound of the shrill voice. It was Mrs Nelson, who had promised their mother to keep an eye on them while she was at work. Tears of defeat pricked Beverley's eyes. When her Mum and Dad got to hear about this she would probably never be allowed to play out again till she got married.

Beverley, after wondering whether to shout to Mrs Nelson to mind her own rotten business and take to her heels with the gargoyle following, gave up the idea. The stupid thing would probably trip up on its coat and fall over, breaking every flagstone in the street.

Then they were saved. Mrs Nelson, peering short-sightedly from her doorstep, gave a gasp of surprise.

'Oh! I didn't know you were with them, Mrs Lee! I *am* sorry. I thought they were on their own.' The street was dark, and without her glasses Mrs Nelson had mistaken the gargoyle for Christine's granny.

'Is your relative better then, Mrs Lee?' asked Mrs Nelson, flustered at her supposed mistake.

'Nod!' hissed Beverley.

The gargoyle ponderously nodded.

'Oh, I am glad. I suppose she wasn't as ill as you thought, then?'

There was another hiss from Beverley and the gargoyle's great heavy head swayed from side to side.

'No, well, I am glad.' Mrs Nelson repeated. She was still rather embarrassed and anxious to end the conversation. 'Well – good night!'

She waved and popped hastily back indoors, shutting the door behind her. Luckily she did not see the gargoyle's answering wave, with three inches of coat sleeve flapping over the end of its stubby hands.

'Come on,' Beverley whispered urgently, and the four of them went as fast as they could to the end of the road. They could not go *too* quickly. Whenever the gargoyle worked itself up to anything like a run, its feet made a noise like two small sledgehammers and the ground shook.

The only other incident which gave them any alarm on the way to the park was when Kevin woke up and began to scream his surprise at finding himself out at night instead of in his cot at home.

'There, there,' said Christine kindly, bending down to comfort him. He yelled all the louder.

'The rotten little thing,' muttered Beverley, who couldn't stand babies. She vaguely suspected that Kevin was misbehaving deliberately in order to get her into trouble. Then, behind Beverley, Kevin caught sight of the hideous stone monster. His face broke into a beaming smile.

'He likes the gargoyle,' said Beverley. 'Put down the hood of the pushchair and let the gargoyle push him. That will shut him up.'

The gargoyle clamped its great stone hands on the handle of the pushchair and, while Beverley and Christine trailed alongside, it steadily wheeled Kevin, now chuckling and happy, to the gates of Hannock Park.

'Oh, no,' said Christine in dismay as they stopped outside. 'The gates are padlocked!'

'Of course they are,' scowled Beverley. 'What do you expect? It's ten o'clock at night.' She shot a quick glance up and down the road. Nobody was about. 'Gargoyle,' she ordered, 'Break the chain.'

The gargoyle shuffled out from behind Kevin's pushchair, grinning amiably.

'But that's Council property, Beverley!' gasped Christine. 'It can't —' There was a sound like snapping cotton, and the chain and padlock lay broken on the ground at their feet.

' – Can't do that,' mumbled Christine, following the others into Hannock Park.

When they reached the middle of the park they made the gargoyle take off its coat and stand between the other statues.

'You can spot it a mile off,' Christine said unhelpfully, and it was true. Even in the darkness the squat and ugly figure stood out like a sore thumb.

Suddenly Christine was struck by something which had been nagging at the back of her mind all night. There was something odd about the monster, something lacking. It was different from how it had looked when they first saw it on the church tower. What was missing?

'Beverley,' she said suddenly. 'Where are its wings?'

'I don't know,' said Beverley uncertainly. She stood rooted to the spot, deep in thought. 'Here, Christine,' she said with dawning excitement. 'The gargoyle – it came to your house about twenty minutes after it went dark!'

'Did it?' said Christine, puzzled.

'Yes, so Christine – *it couldn't have walked!* Not even the gargoyle could walk fifty miles in twenty minutes! Well don't you see?' Beverley's eyes were bright now, 'it must have flown!'

'Oh,' said Christine.

'Well that's it!' shouted Beverley. 'You don't tell it to *go* home, you say – Gargoyle! *Fly* home!'

There was a noise like the grinding of stones. Out of the gargoyle's humped back spread the two black, jagged stone wings that had been folded there. It rolled its marble eyes. The wings beat the air once, twice, fanning a breeze that the two girls could feel where they stood.

The gargoyle nodded farewell to Beverley, flickering its tongue like lightning in and out of its mouth. Then it stretched up its arms, beat the air again with its huge wings and suddenly soared upwards, dwindled to a dot in the sky and finally vanished altogether among the black clouds.

'It's gone,' said Beverley, with a curious note of sadness in her voice. 'It's gone back.'

Christine ran over the grass and picked up her grandmother's coat and umbrella where the gargoyle had left them. 'Yes, and it's taken my Gran's rainhat with it,' she said crossly. 'Oh well, never mind. Come on Beverley, let's get home before Mum finds out.'

When Mrs Lee came back, the house was tidy and everything appeared to be in order. Kevin was fast asleep in his cot and the girls were in bed. Only

Beverley was awake, and she opened her eyes as Mrs Lee tiptoed into the bedroom.

'Everything all right?' she whispered to Beverley. 'Do you want the light left on? No? That's a sensible girl. There's nothing to be afraid of in the dark, is there? Goodnight, Beverley.'

'Goodnight, Mrs Lee.' As Beverley dropped into a deep sleep she thought that if Mrs Lee knew what had happened that night, she might change her mind about that last remark, but naturally she didn't tell her.

The girls never told anyone.

By the time Christine's grandmother discovered the torn lining of her coat, she did not connect it with the night she had gone away to visit her relation. By the time Kevin grew old enough to talk, he thought the whole thing must have been a dream. By the time Mrs Lee noticed that the dog's bowl and two glasses had vanished, Beverley Riley had replaced them.

When the Vicar of Church Milton realised that someone had decorated the ancient gargoyle on the tower with a lady's rainhat, he blamed it on the students of a nearby university playing pranks.

Long afterwards, Beverley and Christine wondered why the spell had taken effect.

'It probably would have worked whoever said the charm,' Christine suggested, but Beverley was inclined to believe that accidentally letting a drop of her blood fall on the gargoyle at the crucial point in the charm had really done the trick.

'One thing's for sure,' she said. 'We're never going to try it again, to find out!'

Decorating the ancient tower of a country church there squats a heavy, ugly statue, its chin resting on its hand and its great black wings spreading from its huge shoulders. It stares over the fields and the rolling hills with its marble eyes, as it has stared for ages past, as it will stare forever unless it is again awoken by a certain magic charm.

The remains of a lady's hat flutter about its stone head, and perhaps its carved grin is a little wider now than when the craftsman fashioned it, all those centuries ago.

The Mysterious Barricades

Joan Aiken

The main thing about the mountains was their height. They were so high that they really did seem to join on to the sky; if you looked at them you had to tip your head back and back until your neck ached; then you were obliged to lie down so that your eyes might go on travelling up to the final snow-crowned summits which were like needles among the clouds.

The people in the village never looked up at them. They had had enough gazing at mountains when they were babies and lay on their backs in prams. As soon as they could walk they turned away from white peaks and dark forests and staggered off in the other direction, towards the plains. If they had to walk towards the mountains they kept their eyes on their boots.

One day a man on a bicycle came to the village. He was a stranger, and consequently everyone stopped work and looked at him, but furtively. The blacksmith put down his hammer, but picked up a piece of string and pretended to be untying it, with his eyes fixed on the traveller. The postman stood gazing at a letter that he had been about to slip into a box as if he had suddenly forgotten how to read. The innkeeper came out on to his balcony and began busily polishing and repolishing a glass, though everyone knew that half the time he didn't trouble to wash them at all.

The traveller pedalled slowly along, glancing from side to side. He saw that every house had someone standing in its doorway or leaning from its window. Only one house seemed to take no interest in him; it was a small bungalow with the name 'Mountain View' painted on its gate. All its windows were lace-curtained and the door was tight shut. He put on his brakes and came to a stop outside it. All the heads craned out a little further to see what he was doing. He leaned his bicycle against the garden wall, unlatched the gate, walked up the path, and rapped at the door.

After a few moments it was opened, and a voice snapped: 'Well, come in, come in. Don't keep me waiting in the cold.'

He hurriedly stepped into the dark interior. He could see hardly anything at first, except the glow of a fire. Both windows had ranks of dark, spreading pot-plants across them, as well as the lace curtains, and bird cages hung in front of the plants. It was very quiet inside; he could hear the clock tick, and the fire rustle, and the birds clearing their throats.

'Well,' said the old woman who had let him in. 'What have you come bothering me for? Aren't there enough busybodies in the village but you have to come and trouble someone who keeps herself to herself?'

'I thought I was more likely to hear the truth from someone who keeps herself to herself,' said the traveller. 'When was the last stranger seen in this village?'

'Ten years ago last Tuesday.'

'And where did he go?'

'He went up the mountains.'

'Did he have a canary and a roll of music with him?'

'As to a roll of music, I can't say; he had a big leather case. He certainly had a canary.'

As she said this one of the birds in the cages began to hop up and down, twittering in a very excited manner.

'Is that the one?' asked the man, looking at it attentively.

'Yes, that's him. Pip, I call him. The man gave him to me for a cup of tea.'

The traveller walked over to the cage, unlatched the door, and whistled a few bars of a tune. The canary continued the tune to its end, finishing with a triumphant trill, and then hopped out on to the man's shoulder.

'He seems to know you,' said the old woman. 'But he's mine for all that.'

The man pulled a cup of tea out of his pocket and handed it to her.

'I'll buy him back off you,' he said. 'Can you tell me anything more? What did this man look like?'

'He had glasses. And a tie like yours. He went off to the mountains and that was the last we saw of him. Ten years is a long time.'

She drank the tea, looking at him thoughtfully.

'I've been ten years tracing him,' said the traveller. 'He stole my canary and he stole my music. I'll go on now, and thank you kindly for the information.'

He tucked the canary into a pocket so that only its head showed, and moved to the door.

'Wait a minute,' said the old woman. 'In return for the tea I'll give you a warning. Those mountains are dangerous. No one who goes up them comes back again. They say there are animals up there with huge feet who can fly faster than the wind.'

'I can't help that, I have to go on,' the traveller said.

'The other man said that too,' the old woman muttered, shaking her head. 'He talked about some mysterious barricades he wanted to find.'

'Yes? In these mountains?' exclaimed the traveller, his face alight with interest and excitement.

'How should I know? It's only what he said. I've never heard of any mysterious barricades – nor do I know what they are, for that matter.'

'They are where the Civil Servants go when they retire,' he told her absently, and he thoughtfully fingered the black and red necktie he wore, which appeared to be made of typewriter ribbon. 'Well, many thanks once more.'

He walked down to the gate and threw one leg over his bicycle.

'You'll never get up the mountains on that,' she called. 'Better leave it here.'

'This machine has a thirty-three speed,' he called back. 'It goes up any hill that isn't vertical,' and he pedalled slowly off. The villagers watched him until he was past them, then they stopped looking in case they should catch a glimpse of the mountains, and went across to question the old woman about her visitor.

But – 'He's been in the Civil Service,' was all she would say, shortly.

'Civil Service!' They looked at their boots, spat, and went off to their own homes.

Meanwhile, the traveller had reached the foot of

the great forest which cloaked the lower slopes of the mountains. He switched to the second of his thirty-three speeds, turned on his light, and pedalled boldly upwards. The road was good, although carpeted with pine needles as if it was rarely used. Far overhead the trees sighed to each other, and above them the out-thrust elbows of the mountain hung over his head.

Soon he came to snow, and the bicycle began to slip and stagger on the frozen crust. He took out chains from the saddlebag and painstakingly laced them round his wheels. This helped his progress, but he was now going more slowly, and night was falling; in the pinewood it was already almost pitch dark. He decided to halt for the night, and leaned his bicycle against a tree. Taking out a groundsheet from the bag he hung it over the bicycle making a rude tent, into which he crawled. From his pocket he drew out another cup of tea and a biscuit. He drank the tea, shared the biscuit with the canary, and then settled himself to sleep.

He had been sleeping for perhaps two hours when he was woken by a terrible howling in the woods above him. It sounded almost like a human cry, but a thousand times louder and more mournful.

He started to his feet, upsetting the bicycle and groundsheet. He saw that it must have been snowing heavily while he slept, for all his footprints were gone and the groundsheet was covered several inches thick. All was silent again, and he moved cautiously a few feet from his encampment, turning his head this way and that to listen. Something caught his eye – a footprint – and he went over to look at it. It made him turn pale.

It was the print of an animal's paw, but what a size! He could have fitted his own foot into it four times over. When he looked for others he saw that they led in a single trail, fifteen feet apart, in a wide ring round his tent, and then away up the hill.

'Perhaps it has gone, whatever it is,' he thought hopefully, but in the same instant he heard the terrible voice again, nearer than before. It seemed to lament, and also to threaten; it echoed among the trees until he could not tell from which quarter it came, and he fled back to his tree and cowered by the bicycle, looking haggardly in all directions. His canary had fallen into a terrified cheeping.

Then his pride began to stir.

'Come,' he said to himself. 'I am a Civil Servant. What would the lower grades think if they saw me now? What would my Administrator think? And he recited to himself the little rhyme which the juniors in the lowest grades are set to learn when they first join the ranks of the Service.

'Always helpful, never hurried,
Always willing, never worried,
Serve the public, slow but surely,
Smile, however sad or poorly,
Duty done without a swerve is
Aimed at by the Civil Service.'

This encouraged him, and as he saw no prospect of further sleep he packed up his ground sheet once more, shared a few biscuit crumbs with the canary and wheeled the bicycle back to the path. He changed down to his thirtieth gear and started to ride up the hill.

Once again he heard the voice reverberating through the trees and seeming to cry: 'Woe! Oh, woe, woe.'

He ducked his head over the handlebars and pedalled on, reciting to himself: Grade I, Step I ten pounds a year. Step II, ten pounds twelve shillings. Step III, ten pounds fifteen shillings. Step IV, ten pounds nineteen shillings. Step V, ten pounds nineteen and six. Grade II, Step I, eleven pounds a year. What a very peculiar tree that is over there. I wonder why there is no snow on it? Annual ex gratia allowances for married men, wife, ten shillings. First child, five shillings. Every subsequent child, two and six. There's another tree on the other side, just the same shape.'

He disliked the two trees which grew along the ground for some distance before turning upwards. They were so very black and so very symmetrical, on either side of the road. An unpleasant fancy came to him that they might be *legs* – but whoever heard of legs the size of pine trees? And if they were legs, where was the body that belonged to them?

He glanced up fearfully into the thickness of the branches above. The sky was beginning to pale with dawn around the edge of the forest, but overhead hung a dense mass of black, supported, it seemed, on those pillar-like trees. He put one foot on the ground and craned back, trying in vain to decide if it was merely the darkness of foliage or if there was something huge leaning over him? As he looked it seemed to move and draw downward, and all at once he saw two great pale eyes, mournful and menacing, descending on him.

With a frantic spasm of courage he flung the bicycle into twenty-second gear and pushed off. He felt a hot dry breath on his neck and struggled desperately up the hill, his heart almost bursting. The light grew ahead and in a few moments he was out of the trees, crashing across virgin snow with the rising sun striking warmly on the top of his head as he bent forward.

He could hear no sound behind, and finally ventured to stop and turn round. Nothing was visible except a distant agitation among the tree tops as if the creature was watching him from the cover of the forest but dared not come out. Encouraged by this he hurried on and was soon out of sight of the trees round a fold of the mountain.

All that day he climbed, and in the green light of evening he was nearing the top of a pass which seemed to cut right through the peak of the mountain. Huge rock walls, seamed with snow, reared up on either side of him.

The traveller was terribly tired. He had hardly halted all day and had eaten nothing save a cup of tea and a biscuit when he paused to pump up his tyres. He had sweated under the fierce heat of noon, but now it was beginning to freeze again and he shivered and longed to lie down and cover himself with the friendly snow.

It seemed to be only a few hundred yards now to the top, and making a final effort he struggled up in ninth gear, to stop aghast at what he saw. The right-hand wall of the pass dropped away at the top, giving a fearful vista of snowy and cloud-wrapped peaks; but the left-hand cliff continued sheering up more and more steeply until it was vertical, with its top veiled in obscurity. Across the face of the cliff ran a narrow ledge – all that remained of the path.

For a moment the traveller was daunted and his heart sank. He had been sure that the top of the pass was the end of his journey and that there he would find the Mysterious Barricades. But his courage only faltered for a short space, and soon he began doggedly working his way along the little path. At first it was wide enough to ride on, but presently he came to a sharp corner in the cliff and he had to dismount. He tried to edge the bicycle round but it slipped from his grasp on the icy rock, and fell outwards. He leaned sideways, holding on to a projection in the cliff and saw the bicycle falling down and down. It became as small as a moth, then as small as a tea-leaf, and finally vanished without the faintest sound coming back to him from the gulf.

He turned, sick and shaken, to continue his journey on foot, but to his unutterable astonishment found the path ahead blocked by another traveller. A short man, wearing spectacles and carrying a leather case stood gazing at him seriously.

The traveller stood silent for a long time.

'Jones!' he said, at length. 'I never expected to meet you here. I thought that you would have passed through the Mysterious Barricades many years ago, using my music as a passport.'

Jones shook his head.

'For ten years I have been wandering in these mountains,' he said sadly. 'I am beginning to believe that the Mysterious Barricades do not exist. I thought that your music would open all gates, but though I have played it daily upon my flute there has been no sign. Perhaps that was the punishment for my theft.'

'How have you lived?' asked the other, looking at him compassionately.

'Buns. They were all I was entitled to, as a Civil Servant Grade III. Would you care for one? I am sick of the sight of them.'

'I'll give you a cup of tea for it.'

'Tea!' Jones's eyes lit up. 'I didn't know you had reached the higher grades.' He drank it as if it was nectar, while the other man munched his bun, pleasantly filling after a prolonged diet of biscuit.

'Now what are we to do?' said Jones presently. 'We cannot pass each other on this ledge and if one of us tries to turn round he will probably be dashed to destruction.'

'Let us play my sonata for two flutes and continuo,' said the traveller, who had been looking at the leather portfolio for some minutes past.

Jones cautiously drew out some sheets of manuscript music and passed them over. The traveller turned through them until he came to the piece he wanted, which was inscribed: 'Sonata in C major for two flutes and continuo by A. Smith.'

The two men took out their flutes and Smith propped his manuscript on a ledge in the cliff face so that they could see it by looking sideways. They stood facing each other and played the sonata through, but when they came to the end nothing happened.

'It wants the continuo part,' said Smith sadly. 'Let us play it again and I will try to put it in.'

They began again, though Jones looked doubtful.

This time the canary suddenly popped its head from Smith's pocket, where it had been sleeping, and began to sing with its eyes fixed on the distant peaks and its throat filling and emptying like the bellows of an organ. The two players gazed at each other over their flutes in astonishment but nothing would have made them stop playing, for the music produced by the two flutes and the bird was of more than mortal beauty. As they played the mountains trembled about them; great slabs of snow dislodged from their niches and slipped into the gulf, spires of rock trembled and tottered, and as the travellers came to the end of the sonata, the Mysterious Barricades opened to receive them.

Down below the villagers felt the ground quiver as they trudged homewards with the sugar beet harvest, and their tractors snorted and belched blue smoke. But the men never lifted their eyes from the ground, and the women turned their backs to the windows, so none of them saw the strange things that were happening in the mountains.

The Bungling Bunyip

Pamela Vincent

There was once an Australian bunyip who made a very good job of being scary. In fact, he was so good at it that at night no one ever came near the rather pleasant billabong* where he lived.

It was a very lonely life because night-time is when a bunyip is wide awake, ready to have fun, and it's no fun being scary if you can't see someone being scared. In fact, sometimes the dreadful noise that kept everyone away was just the bunyip moaning to himself about how bored he was.

One day, as the sun was going down, a big square box of a car lumbered to the edge of the billabong and parked under the few thin trees. A man and woman got out and a girl and a boy followed them. The children proceeded to help the man set up a couple of tents while the woman prepared a meal.

The bunyip watched with interest. He had never seen people close to before because he was always asleep in the daytime, but he knew what these creatures were – long ago he remembered his old mother telling him about them, and how tasty they were –

* A pool left by a dried-up river.

126

especially the young ones. He thought he would watch them for a while before eating them, as he might never have another chance to see what human beings did to pass the time, and it was really quite interesting.

Night comes quickly in the north of Australia, and soon the colours of sunset gave way to a vast, clear sky filled with stars that were almost near enough to touch. The family finished their meal and tidied up so that there was no rubbish left to spoil their camp site, and the bunyip thought perhaps it was time for him to start scaring them. He opened his mouth, ready to make the night hideous with a great roar, but, at that very moment there came a noise he had never heard before. He closed his mouth and listened.

After a time, he found his head wagging and his toes tapping. It was a very noisy noise but he liked it! It seemed to come from a box that the children fed other little oblong boxes into.

'That's enough, kids,' said the man, at last. 'Time for some shut-eye so that we can make an early start tomorrow.'

'Oh, Dad, not yet,' cried the girl. 'I don't feel a bit sleepy, do you, Graham?'

'I won't go to sleep for *hours*,' said her brother, firmly.

'Well, I'm going to bed even if you want to stay awake all night,' yawned their mother, 'but don't tell me how tired you are tomorrow, that's all.'

'They can sleep in the car tomorrow,' said their father. 'It won't do them any harm to stay up a bit longer out in the fresh air while they're on holiday.'

'Being bitten by things,' said his wife, scratching.

The bunyip smiled to himself. 'Bitten by *me*,' he thought, happily. 'Quite soon now.'

The parents disappeared inside their tent and the children sat listening to a million frogs who lived around the billabong and didn't mind the bunyip. The bunyip decided that his moment had come and this time he gave one of his best bellows.

'What on earth was that?' asked Karen, not sounding a bit scared.

'Oh, frogs, I expect,' answered Graham. 'They make a lot of funny noises.'

Funny? The bunyip was indignant. Funny indeed! He'd show them!

'There it is again,' said Karen.

'I wish it would shut up,' said her brother. 'It's going to wake Mum and Dad.'

The bunyip thought it was time to scare them properly. With heavy footfalls he splashed through the water and squelched through the mud, rustling the thin bushes and trees.

'That's not a frog,' remarked Karen.

'It can't be the wind,' said Graham. 'There isn't any.'

'It isn't,' roared the bunyip, close to them. 'It's ME!'

'It's I,' corrected Karen, without thinking, then added, 'Who said that?'

'I did,' said the bunyip, sulkily. These children should have been running away, screaming in fright by now, so that he could chase them.

'Who are you? I can't see anyone,' said Graham.

'I'm a bunyip,' answered the bunyip, waiting for them to start running.

'A what?' asked Karen. 'A bunny?'

'Bunyip. B-U-N-Y-I-P.' The bunyip spelt it out.

'What's that?' asked Graham.

'I'm a monster who eats children,' snapped the bunyip, annoyed.

'Oh, one of those,' yawned Graham. 'A sort of bogeyman. You don't really exist.'

The bunyip's jaw dropped in astonishment.

'Of course I exist,' he exclaimed. 'What do you think I'm doing here?'

'I don't know, I can't see you.'

'You'll know when I eat you,' said the bunyip, gnashing his teeth.

'Oh, please don't grind your teeth like that,' begged Karen, shuddering. 'Why don't you come out and show yourself?'

'Because I'm invisible.'

'You can't eat us with an invisible mouth,' Graham pointed out.

'It's no use expecting us to believe in you if we can't see you,' said Karen, 'so if you'll excuse us we'll go to bed now.'

'No, wait — ' The bunyip felt it was important for the children to believe in him.

'I'm sorry, but I don't like talking to someone who isn't there,' said Karen.

'But I *am* here,' insisted the bunyip.

'Then show us what you look like – or are you too ugly?' asked Graham.

The bunyip suddenly realised that he didn't *know* what he looked like.

'I don't think he knows how to make himself visible,' said Graham, unkindly.

'I do too!'

The bunyip cast his mind back several centuries to what his old mother had told him before she'd gone walkabout and never come back, and although he was a bit rusty, he made a big effort and created a shadowy body that the children could just make out by the light of the moon that had risen a little while ago.

'You're not a bunyip,' cried Karen, 'you're a kangaroo!'

The bunyip looked down at himself (it was easier for him to see in the half-dark because he was more used to it than the children). He *did* look like a kangaroo. But then he knew what kangaroos looked like and he didn't know what bunyips looked like.

'Kangaroos are nice,' said Karen, stroking his head and fondling his ears.

'I'm not a kangaroo and I'm not nice,' snapped the bunyip, fiercely, feeling rather foolish. 'I'm a monster that eats children!'

'*You're* not very nice,' agreed Karen, 'but you look like a kangaroo and a kangaroo wouldn't eat us – he couldn't eat us, in fact.'

'In fact,' added Graham, thoughtfully, 'we might eat *you*.'

The bunyip shivered in his fur and took a deep breath, trying to imagine himself as an old-time dragon. Karen jumped back in fright, then leaned forward again to peer at him. She had to look down at him, a long way down.

'I'm not sure but I think you've turned into a goanna,' she said, beginning to feel sorry for the bunyip.

A goanna does look a bit like a dragon. All lizards do and a goanna is a big lizard, but a dragon half a metre long is no more scary than a kangaroo – or an invisible bunyip.

'You'll have to do better than that,' scoffed Graham.

'Maybe you're extinct,' suggested Karen. 'You know, like the dodo and the unicorn and other things that used to live in the world but don't any more.'

Tears rolled down the bunyip's goanna face and

the children felt ashamed of their teasing.

'I might as well be extinct if no one's scared of me,' wept the bunyip. 'There's no place in the world for an unscary monster, and I'm so lonely here anyway.'

'I'll tell you what,' offered Graham. 'You make yourself invisible again and we'll tell everybody that you're a big, fearsome monster but you've given up eating people. Then people will come here to be scared (but not eaten) and they'll enjoy themselves whilst you'll have some company.'

And so it was. When Graham and Karen went back home they told their friends about the bunyip's billabong and every weekend there would be picnics and barbecues followed by a scary performance from the bunyip in the moonlight or the starlight. He loved to hear the music of cassette-players and then the screams of fright as he roared and howled and shrilled, and splashed and squelched through the billabong, and rustled and hustled on invisible, stomping feet – or were they paws, or hooves? Nobody waited to find out, they all scattered before he reached the camp sites. The bunyip didn't mind – he found that the food human beings brought with them tasted much nicer than human beings themselves.

First Performance

Geoffrey Palmer and Noel Lloyd

When Abraham Benz, the great German composer, died a few years ago, music-lovers all over the world were sad, though no one was very surprised, for he was ninety-seven when the event occurred.

Benz had been famous for his eccentric behaviour as well as for his music. He had quarrelled with other composers, with conductors, singers and orchestras. He had walked out of concerts of his own music, and once he had interrupted the performance of one of his operas with a demand for the leading soprano to 'keep to the tune I wrote'. Everybody had a story to tell of his outrageous actions, yet at the same time he was loved by a great number of once-struggling singers and musicians to whom he had given either advice, encouragement or money.

His music was admired without reservation. He had written symphonies, concertos, songs, operas – even the occasional pop song (under an assumed name) when he needed money quickly to help one of his deserving causes. So when, a few months after his death, his stepson, the conductor Franz Freiden, announced that he had found a new symphony among Benz's papers, the musical world hummed with excitement. It was likely to be one of Benz's major works, Freiden said, and was certainly the longest. The excitement grew when it became known that the first performance would be given in London and that it would be conducted by Freiden himself.

It was common knowledge that Benz had always disliked Freiden, and that Freiden had considered his stepfather to be a silly old man, but this did not worry anybody. The concert would be a musical occasion of the first importance, and everybody who *was* anybody was determined to be present, as well as several thousand members of the general public.

London's largest concert hall was sold out two hours after the bookings opened, and a great success was predicted for Benz's Fifteenth Symphony. Such was the enthusiasm that the entire audience had taken their seats several minutes before the concert began. There were no latecomers, no stragglers who had lingered over their coffees in the foyer. The members of the orchestra lost no time in getting to their places: they tuned their instruments immediately, then waited for Franz Freiden to arrive.

As soon as he appeared, a tall, spruce figure with a shock of grey hair, the applause broke the silence like a sudden thunderclap. Freiden walked briskly to the rostrum, acknowledged the applause with a grave nod, then, with baton raised, faced the players. The last cough was stifled, the last programme rustled. With a neat gesture Franz Freiden brought the symphony to life.

The gently rhythmic tune, played by the violins, violas and cellos, cast an immediate spell. The double basses joined in and gave it greater depth, then the woodwind instruments had their say and after them a single French horn gave it a mellow glow. Freiden, with eyes closed, swayed to the rhythm, carried away by the beauty he was creating. Never had he imagined that any orchestra could play so superbly. It was going to be a performance of supreme perfection . . . .

Freiden knew the music by heart and prepared himself for the coming violent intrusion of the brass and percussion that would change the mood completely. Soon all the instruments except the violins had trembled into silence, and Freiden turned to the violin section, bringing the sound down to a thin, sweet thread. The last few notes were played in unison. It was time for the thread to snap – when suddenly the air was jarred by the sourest, most discordant note that any violin had ever played.

The harsh, unexpected sound brought the violinists to a faltering stop. Freiden screwed up his face in agony. He almost cried out in anger, but controlled himself just in time, and contented himself with a furious glare at the violinists. He tried to identify the culprit. Surely it must have been the one on the back row, the player with the strange mocking grin on his face. He peered closer at the man, then gave a start and almost dropped his baton. Wasn't that – but it couldn't be – it was too ridiculous – and yet – oh, I must be going mad, Freiden thought. He blinked rapidly and shook his head as if to dispel an unpleasant vision, and remembered just in time that the music had to go on.

He turned towards the brass section, opened his arms wide, and gave them the beat for the entry of their martial tune. When it came the hall reverberated with the tremendously exciting noise. It was as if the Day of Judgement had been announced. Magnificent! thought Freiden. Now we can forget that terrible moment . . . .

The tune reached its climax; then it was repeated, first by the trumpets to a background of plucked strings, then by the French horns. The tubas added their version, and a drum roll announced the trombones.

The trombones started beautifully – deep, but with the right touch of hoarseness. But the smoothness of their last sliding notes was interrupted by a crude sound that could only be described as a raspberry . . . .

Again the audience was shaken out of its rapt mood, and a loud murmuring broke out. This time Freiden did drop his baton. In a mixture of rage and despair he shook his fists above his head and uttered a savage exclamation. He cast a withering look at the startled trombonists, then stepped back as though trying to avert an unexpected danger. 'No no – I *must* be going mad,' he muttered. 'It can't be . . . .' He looked again at the trombonists. There had been four. But now there were only three – where had the fourth one gone? He could have sworn there were four when he mounted the rostrum.

He leaped off his rostrum and pushed his way to the back of the orchestra. 'Vhere, vhere, vhere? You, you and you – vhere is he?'

The leader of the orchestra hurried up to him. 'Mr Freiden, please calm down.' He started to pat the conductor on the shoulder, making ineffectual noises.

But Freiden was not to be soothed. 'He's hiding somewhere, ze old – how you say – cheat!' he gasped. He approached the first trombone with such a menacing look in his eyes that the player stretched out the slide of his instrument to the full to keep him at bay. 'Vhere you hide him, eh?'

'I'm not hiding nobody,' the first trombone twittered, forgetting his grammar in the heat of the moment.

'Ach,' said Freiden and pushed past more players until he reached the tympanist. 'Let me look behind your tymp, eh? Perhaps you hide him.'

'Who, m-me?' the tympanist asked, with a sickly grin.

Freiden wriggled his way between the three kettle-drums and addressed the other percussion players. 'Vhere he hide? Beneath your drum – under ze glockenspiel? I must find him . . . .'

While all this was going on the people in the hall, shattered first by the music and then by its bizarre sequel, were pushing and struggling to get a better view of the fantastic proceedings. The members of the orchestra were adding to the confusion by arguing excitedly among themselves about what had happened.

Freiden blundered about the platform like a maddened bull, knocking over chairs and upsetting music stands in his attempt to locate the mysterious fourth trombonist. Vainly the leader appealed to the players to sit down and be calm, and in the auditorium the stewards were doing their best to restore order. The manager of the hall and the orchestra manager, together with their assistants, had appeared on the platform and were chasing after the frantic conductor like huntsmen in full cry after a fox; and a flustered nurse, clutching a bottle of sal volatile, brought up the rear.

At last Freiden was surrounded by his pursuers and he disappeared in the scrum. When he emerged, dusty and tousled, all the fight had gone out of him.

He was dusted down and consoled. He was promised that a searching enquiry would be held and that the practical joker who had been responsible for the disturbance would be severely dealt with. After a great deal of muttering and head-shaking he agreed to continue with the concert. He made his way back to the rostrum to a burst of applause from the audience, a rather hysterical sound made up of relief that the concert was going to be resumed and gratitude for the unexpected entertainment they had witnessed.

Freiden decided to start again from the entry of the brass. This time the notorious trombone passage went off without a hitch and in a short time the music had woven its spell round all the eager listeners.

With a great sweeping movement the conductor launched the players into the last great tune of the movement. It swirled thrillingly through the hall like a waterfall cascading down a mountainside. Then he alerted the orchestra for the two pauses that punctuated the end of the movement. The flood of sound was halted for a count of three. There was another climax, another pause before the last breath-taking chord. The first pause was perfection; the silence could almost be felt. The re-entry of the orchestra was like a mighty shout of triumph. Freiden brought his baton down for the second pause. One – two – and on the third beat the silence was broken by a clear, piping 'Cuckoo!'

In the pandemonium that followed all hope of further music that evening dwindled and disappeared. Freiden hurled his baton from him and, roaring at the top of his voice, stamped off the platform and made his way blindly to the conductor's room. There he locked the door and burst into tears.

Eventually the doors of the concert hall were closed against the last reluctant newspaper reporter. Back-stage, the musicians had been questioned about the events of the evening, but no explanation of the interpolations that had ruined Benz's symphony was forthcoming. All the violinists vigorously denied having caused the sour note; the three trombonists were positive that the raspberry had not come from them and everybody was insistent that the cuckoo sound had not come from any of their instruments. Yet the sounds had been made – but by whom?

The manager allowed the musicians to leave. 'I suppose it could be a conspiracy,' he said to his assistant, 'but why should anyone deliberately try to ruin such an important occasion?' With a baffled groan he went to the conductor's room and knocked on the door. 'Please let me come in, Herr Freiden,' he pleaded.

'Go avay,' came a muffled shout from the conductor. 'I vill not come out from here – ever! I am disgraced – ruined – nobody vill ever vant me to conduct again!'

It was long after midnight when they gave up hope of persuading him to change his mind. 'We'll just have to let him stay until he comes to his senses,' the manager said. 'Perhaps when he's really hungry he'll decide he's had enough solitary confinement. Anyway, I'm going home. Goodness knows what my wife will say . . . .' He turned to the chief steward. 'Mr Bulstrode, I'm going to leave you in charge. You'd better stay here till something happens – if anything does.'

'That's all right, sir,' said Mr Bulstrode cheerfully. 'Poor chap, I can understand how he feels. I locked myself in the kitchen once when I thought I'd won the pools and then found I'd forgotten to post the coupon. Terrible, it was. I've got over it now, but —'

'Yes, yes,' said the manager hastily. 'Quite. Well, I must be off . . .'

So everyone went home and the chief steward was left alone with the heartbroken conductor. He tapped at the door and called out, 'Would you like a nice cup of tea, sir, and maybe a digestive biscuit? The kettle's on – I'll have it made in a couple of shakes.'

He waited, head on one side, but there was no reply. 'Well, I could do with a cuppa meself, seeing as how it's going to be an all-night sitting,' he muttered, and ambled off to his room in the basement.

When all was still, the door of the conductor's room opened slowly and a white-faced Freiden peeped out. He made his way carefully along the dimly lit corridor and entered the pitch-dark auditorium. When he had found his rostrum he stepped up on to it and gazed into the blackness around him, first towards where the audience had been, and then he turned round as if the orchestra were waiting for his baton to summon them to their task.

Fresh tears came to his eyes. 'Vhy, oh vhy did this have to happen to me?' he cried, then gave a little jump as the echo of his words rumbled round the hall. And as the poor man stood wiping his eyes with a handkerchief, the echo died away and there came from somewhere in the gloom around him a loud, musical, 'Cuckoo!'

Freiden felt the hairs at the back of his neck rise, and he shivered with fear. 'Who – who – is there?' he said in a quavering voice, in his native German.

'Franz, you know very well who is here,' came the answer.

He did know – there was no mistaking the querulous tone, even though it did seem to be echoing in a cavern. His fear disappeared, and he faced where he thought the voice had come from. 'Abraham Benz! Then it was you, stepfather!'

The answer was a chuckle.

'So it was *you*,' Freiden went on bitterly, 'sitting among the violins, grinning like a fiend. *You* were the fourth trombonist. And it was *you* who cried "Cuckoo" . . . .'

'Yes, it was I,' said the voice. 'I did it all rather well, don't you think?'

'But – but you are dead –' Freiden spluttered. 'Then – then it's your ghost who has played these tricks!'

'You may use that term if you like,' the voice said impatiently. 'But I will show you that Abraham Benz is as much alive dead as he was alive!'

And a formless glowing cloud emerged from the back of the hall and slowly moved towards Freiden until it was only a few feet from him. Freiden shrank back, covering his face with his hands. Gradually the glow subsided, the edges of the cloud hardened and took the shape of an old man. Abraham Benz stood before the terrified conductor, apparently as real and solid as he had been in life.

'Look at me,' he commanded.

Freiden let his hands drop. He stared at the ghost of his stepfather.

'Do I look like a ghost?' demanded the old man.

Freiden shook his head. 'But you are . . . Tell me, why did you ruin everything tonight? The music was sublime, the orchestra was playing brilliantly, the occasion would have added still more lustre to your name. Yet the evening ended as a fiasco. I dread to think what the papers will say tomorrow. Why did you do it?'

Abraham Benz's ghost growled. 'Stop playing the fool, man. Use your wits and tell *me* why I stopped the symphony. Why pretend that you don't know?'

Freiden stepped down from the rostrum, groped for a chair and half collapsed on to it. 'I thought nobody would ever find out,' he groaned. 'I know that what I did was wrong – but I *had* to do it. How could I know that you would interfere?'

'Foolish man,' said the ghost. 'Do you understand now that what I did was for your own good?'

'Yes, yes, I see that now. I was mad to think that I could get away with it,' Freiden said humbly.

'If I had not interfered as I did,' the ghost went on, 'the evening would have been a resounding success, as we know. The world would have again acclaimed Abraham Benz. What a genius! they would have said. It is not many composers whose last work is their greatest. That is what they *would* have said. Now the world is going to know the truth.'

Freiden rose to protest, crying 'No, no!' But the ghost moved too and towered above him.

'The world will know that Benz did not write that symphony – that Benz's Fifteenth Symphony is really Franz Freiden's First!'

Freiden spread out his hands in despair. 'How can I explain that *I* wrote the music? Would anyone believe me?'

'That is your problem,' said the ghost. 'But – I warn you – if you ever conduct Benz's so-called Fifteenth again I shall assist you just as I did tonight! But if it is Freiden's First, then I shall be an invisible power at your side, helping you to create the performance of a lifetime. Choose . . .'

'You make it very difficult,' Freiden complained. 'I would never have deceived the public and tried to pass of my work as yours if I had thought its true worth would have been recognised. But who would have come to a concert to hear music by *me?* A handful of my friends, perhaps, and one or two critics convinced in advance that nothing I wrote could be any good. I knew my symphony was good. When I was going through your papers the idea came to me . . . I copied your writing and your musical notation until your style was mine. Then I wrote my own score just as you would have done it. The result – a new symphony by Abraham Benz!'

There was a more sympathetic tone in the ghost's voice. 'You were wrong, though I understand why you acted as you did. A true artist cares nothing for what the critics say. If your music had not been so fine I would not have bothered to interfere. Where I am now fame is not important. But at last *you* have justified yourself by composing music I would have been proud to call my own. After tonight, because of what has happened, your name will be on everyone's lips. You will be besieged by reporters tomorrow, and you will tell them the truth! Then you will give a repeat performance of Freiden's First, and I shall be there – listening . . . .'

'I will do that!' Freiden straightened himself up, his eyes lit up with hope. 'Thank you, dear stepfather —'

But his stepfather was no longer there, and though he strained his eyes through the gloom he could see nothing. 'Where are you?' he called.

The only answer was a faint 'Cuckoo!' that seemed to be coming from the depths of a distant wood.

Mr Bulstrode, the chief steward, nearly dropped his cup of tea when he heard a tap at the door of his basement room and Franz Freiden, tired-looking but happy, stepped over the threshold.

'Ah, my friend,' the conductor said, rubbing his hands together expectantly, 'so I have found you! I think, perhaps, I will accept that cup of tea you offered, if there is still one in the pot, huh?'

The Spooky Thing

William O. Steele

There were once two boys called Gist and Meriweather, and they were as ornery and mean as a
bushel of rattlesnakes. All they ever did was argue
and fight. They no sooner roused up out of bed of a
morning than they'd light in on one another.

And they kept at it the livelong day too. The
wood went uncut, the cows went unmilked, the
corn unhoed. In truth, those two young 'uns just
about pestered the life out of their old pa.

Now, their daddy was a fine sort of man, hard-
working all his life and never did nobody a minute's
harm. And he had a fair-to-middling farm where he
could have made a good living if he'd had any decent
help. Folks felt mighty sorry for him because he had
two trifling sons so all-fired mean they wouldn't
lend their pa a hand with the work.

At one time or another folks had offered him all
sorts of kind advice on how to make those boys
straighten up and act right. And their pa had been so
desperate and long-suffering he was willing to try
just a heap of cures.

So, he had tried thinning the boys' blood with tonics made of tree roots and plant leaves and red earthworms. And he got their blood so thin they about froze to death the first cold frost. But the meanness never left them. It stayed right with them as thick and worrisome as ever.

And their pa had stewed them over a slow fire for two days in a big black pot filled with purple-headed sneezeweed and wild bumblebee feet and a bacon rind or two. Oh– the air was filled with steam for a while, and the boys sort of shrunk up in their skins. Why, they stewed down to a clear syrup, just right for canning or preserving, but the meanness stayed as strong as ever when they were taken out of the pot.

Their pa had tried a heap more salves and herbal teas, but nothing made those boys change their ways. Nothing! And so he gave up trying to cure 'em.

'It's their nature to be mean,' he said, 'and I reckon ain't nothing on earth can make them change their ways.'

However, one day their pa had his fill. He just couldn't stand their fighting and arguing any longer. He craved a day's peace and quiet like a pig craves buttermilk. And the only way he knew to get a day's rest was to send his sons off somewhere.

So, he called them to him. And they came rolling right up to his feet, scuffling and yelling and a-snapping at each other like two fighting wildcats. The noise was so loud their pa had to clap both hands over his ears and a feather bed or two, but that didn't help much. He shouted and ranted, and they never paid him no mind.

Finally he reached down and grabbed them by the scruff of the neck and yanked them apart. And he shook them a time or two in the air and banged their heads together, though it brought most of the rocks in the chimney tumbling down around them. When they had quit snarling at each other, he stood them on the ground before him.

Gist was the oldest and by far the biggest. He had two front teeth missing where his younger brother had been careless enough to hit him with a hoe once when they got to fighting real bad and the younger one was losing. Now, whenever Gist grinned, that gap made him look about as wicked as seven sinners all in a row.

But in truth Gist wasn't any more wicked than his brother. And they both could have given the devil lessons in meanness.

Meriweather was small and quick as a sunny-sided minnow after a tadpole. And his green eyes could shine out bright and hateful when he was feeling mean, which was most of the time. Of course he wasn't handsome one bit, not with that big scar running all jagged and ugly across his forehead from the time Gist pushed him out of the hayloft to give him a chance to fly.

Their pa said, 'I want you boys to go to the settlement and do some trading for me.'

And right then those two young'uns were sweet as honey and brown sugar. Their pa had never before sent them to town by themselves, so they were eager to go.

They did his bidding without faulting one another, and nary a slap nor bite passed between them whilst they were readying themselves for the journey. They never even complained once, though they had to fill up two sacks with dried ginseng roots and hunt through the barn for a length of string to tie up the bags.

'Take them roots and get me a cowskin and as much meat as you can trade for,' their pa told them. 'And don't neither one of you set foot back on this farm till sundown. But mind you, be here then. I don't want you out after dark.'

'Yes, Pa,' they answered in the meekest kind of way, though it most nigh killed them to be nice and polite.

And off they went in the early morning before the birds were winging, while the dew still lay on the meadow deep enough to float a flatboat. The brothers never noticed the wetness nor the last star hanging above the ridge, and it faded away un-wished-on.

They walked straight to the settlement and never said a word to each other along the way, never argued nor sassed one another at all. And they found the town filled to busting with folks, for it was court day. The boys looked about to their hearts' content, did their trading, and in the late afternoon struck out for home.

Gist saw how much meat there was, and he had no mind to fetch it back to the farm himself.

'After all,' he told himself, 'I'm the biggest, and it may be I'll have to twist a good many alligators' tails or kick a few mosquitoes to get them off the path so Meriweather can get by with the meat.'

So before his brother could so much as say 'Boo turkey,' Gist grabbed up the cowskin and slung it across his shoulder. And he set out along the path whistling, happy to have tricked his brother without getting an ear knocked crooked or a toe chewed off.

Meriweather wasn't slow to see what his brother had done to him. And he didn't like it one whit. He didn't like Gist's whistling either. And, for that matter, he didn't like Gist.

But there was nothing in creation for him to do but bide his time. So, he hoisted the heavy load of meat to his shoulder and set out after his brother.

And he kept his eyes sharp for a chance to get even with Gist. It was a thing he was especially good at, Sundays or dog days, at cockcrow or during Blackberry Winter, or just about any time you care to name.

Now Meriweather tried his living best to catch up with his brother. He took short cuts and swung over ridges on grapevines and ran through mole tunnels at breakneck speed. And every single solitary time he got real close, Gist would strike out at a trot and go way ahead again.

This didn't set too well with Meriweather. He got hotter and hotter and madder and madder. And he was just about to split wide open, he hated his brother so all-fired much.

Gist had long since ceased to carry the hide over his shoulder. That had become too much like work. It wasn't that he was lazy. No. But work made him break out in a rash in the worst, itchy sort of way, and he had to be mighty careful.

So, he was going along the path, holding the hide by the tail and a-dragging it along careless-like through the dust with the old skull bone rattling and bumping over stones and roots.

At last the path wound around and around a steep mountain. Meriweather waited till his brother was halfway up. Then he dropped his load of meat and ran up behind his brother on quiet tippytoes and jumped on the hide, hard and fierce.

Gist was taken plumb by surprise and was jerked right smack over on his back with the breath knocked out of him. Whooosh!

But he never let go his hold on the cow's tail. And

Meriweather squeezed his brother's head till it was as flat and soft as a pat of butter, but he couldn't make him turn loose the hide. It was not till Meriweather stomped Gist's knuckles a dozen times or so right hard that his brother agreed it was Meriweather's turn to tote the cowskin.

So, Meriweather grabbed it up, gave his brother a quick shove, and ran off over the hill for home, feeling spry as a chicken in high oats, while Gist went spinning off down the mountainside so fast he was sure that a part of himself had been left behind. He tried to count his arms and legs that went whirling around him. But every now and then a knee or elbow would strike a flint rock and make sparks go flying every which a way, and the pain would be so terrible that Gist would forget what he'd counted.

'Was that 997 legs or 799 arms?' he would ask himself and have to begin all over again.

Finally he reached the bottom and was smashed all over the side of a great big boulder. He felt to see if any bones were broken. He counted his fingers.

'Ten,' he shouted, happy to find them all there.

And then he was so confused he added up his legs and divided by two and decided that he had lost a leg. He was much upset about this. But he had no time to look for the lost leg then.

He marked the place as best he could so that, when he came back to look, he'd know the spot. Then he shouldered the meat and began climbing the hill. And every once in a while he'd stop and shout all sorts of bad names at his brother.

But Meriweather never heard him because he had hurried till he was way out in front. And at last he came to a spring and stopped. He was powerful thirsty.

'I've just got to have a drink of this cool water,' he

said aloud, 'for if I don't, I'll get the dry wobbles and that's a mighty terrible thing for a young boy like me to have.'

He glanced back along the path. Gist was nowhere in sight, so right then and there Meriweather flung the hide aside and flopped down flat on his belly. He drank and drank and drank.

Now Gist had stolen up soft and quiet through the trees. And when he saw his brother with his head in the water, he didn't hold back one minute.

He jumped smack in the middle of Meriweather's back. He pushed his brother's head down under the water and his face deep into the mud, and then Gist laughed a happy, triumphant laugh, for that was the best way in the world to treat a brother.

Meriweather came snorting and splashing up out of that spring, shaking water and mud and dead leaves every which ways. Oh, he was as wet and mad as a well bucket.

And the minute he dug the mud and trash out of his eyes, he picked up a big old rock and let fly at Gist. That rock smacked Gist on the side of the head with a crack that sounded mighty like the world had split in two.

Now Gist didn't want his brother to know he was hurt, and so he ran way back in the mountains before he hollered 'Ouch!'

Then he ran back to where Meriweather was, and they went at it, rocked each other back and forth across that spring till the bushes lay all trampled and twisted and the water was mashed so flat it wasn't fit to drink.

Rocks rattled through the woods like falling hail and filled the air so that the sunlight was shut out. Chickens went to roost, and squinch owls came out and flew around hooting in the dark. Never was there such a rock battle!

At last they were worn to a frazzle from fighting, and they quit. And when the sun came shining back, they were a sight to see, all battered out of shape and with little nicks and chips and notches knocked away and dents and cracked places all over them.

But they weren't so cut up and bruised and sore they couldn't go right on faulting each other.

'I reckon you're sorry you begun that fight,' Gist said, panting hard.

'Never begun it,' retorted Meriweather.

'Did too.'

'Never neither.'

'I reckon I showed you I'm the best fighter,' said Gist. 'Oh, it pleasured me to whup you so good and proper, which is only fair, and it's certainly an older brother's rightful duty.'

'Well, you never bested me. Look at the size of that knot.' And Meriweather laughed and laughed to see how wopsided his brother looked.

Gist felt his head, and he hoped he wouldn't have to hide in any snake holes, for he'd never be able to get in one, the way that knot had swelled out.

'I aim to tell Pa how you acted,' Gist said, grunting. 'I aim to tell him a whole rigamarole about your meanness. And Pa'll whup you so hard your toenails will drop off. And it'll serve you right for starting the fight.'

'Pa might whip me, but you sure ain't never going to,' taunted Meriweather, and he reached out and slashed at his brother with his sharp old fingernail, slicking off a handful of hair and the right sleeve of Gist's shirt.

Gist was on his feet in a wink. 'Why, I'll flail the jelly out of you, right this dang minute,' he yelled. He doubled up his fist and he made straight for

Meriweather.

But Meriweather pointed to the west. 'Sun's a-setting,' he said, 'We'd best hurry if we aim to get home by sundown.'

He leaped for the cow's hide, but Gist beat him to it.

'No, you don't,' Gist hollered. 'My time to tote the skin, yours the meat.' And off he trotted with the hide.

And so the two of them went along in the twilight with their burdens and their meanness, on through clouds of gnats and puddles of knee-deep dust. They panted and they puffed and they hurried something awful.

But dark came and caught them a mighty far piece from the farm. Ahead of them was the woods, black and scary-looking and no fit place for two helpless boys to be travelling by themselves.

'If you didn't poke along so slow, we'd have been home by now,' complained Gist, for it was his bounden duty to point out his brother's many weaknesses. But mostly he just wanted to drop back and wait for his brother to catch up with him. Gist didn't aim to go any farther by himself, for he had never seen the woods so tarnal dark and dreary. And woods at night was sure one thing that didn't agree with him.

Meriweather came up and said, 'Your time with the meat.'

'Nope, it ain't,' answered the older.

''Tis too.'

''Tain't neither.'

And so they passed among the dark trees, arguing and calling one another names and giving each other swats and pinches, but staying mighty close together just the same, for all they hated one another.

Finally Gist said he could go no farther. He lay down to rest. Meriweather stopped too, making sure his load of meat fell on his brother's foot.

'Yowwww!' screamed Gist, grabbing his foot. 'You done that a-purpose.'

Meriweather smiled wickedly to himself and sank down into the leaves beside his brother.

They rested there for a spell, and the trees closed in around them, black and tall. It was mighty quiet and still there in the gloom. And yet all kinds of creatures seemed to be running around them in the shadows, a-whispering strange things to each other.

The brothers edged closer and closer together, so close the fog creeping up from the river could not part them. And when Gist shook, Meriweather's teeth rattled, and when Meriweather's knees knocked together, Gist's head joggled about all loose and squeaky.

'I'm famished clean through to my backbone,' said Meriweather. 'Gist, let's roast a piece of that meat. We're already late, and a little bit longer won't matter none.'

'Can't have no fire,' answered his brother. 'I never brought my flint and steel.'

Meriweather was just about to hit him a good lick for being so forgetful when he spied something. 'I believe to my soul I see a fire up there in that tree,' he cried.

He rubbed his eyes and looked again. Sure enough, there it was still, a heap of burning coals up in a tree.

'I'll just shinny up there and get it,' he said.

'I'll let you,' answered Gist, 'for I'm much too busy to go myself.'

So Meriweather began to climb the tree, and it wasn't any time at all till he was near the bright red embers. And then he reached out his hand to pick up a coal.

Suddenly he saw it wasn't a fire there but a THING crouched on the limb!

What he thought was embers was its red old eyes. And he was close enough to see its teeth gleaming knife-sharp and big as chopping axes, which wasn't a sight to cheer up a body. Its carcass was all wrinkled and full of thorny bunches of bristles here and there, and it sat on that limb in a funny folded-up sort of way.

'What ye want with me?' the THING asked.

Now, Meriweather was powerful scared and shaky, but he wasn't so taken aback his wits wouldn't work. He spoke up as quick and as pleasant as he was able on such short notice.

'My brother said come down and get yourself some meat to eat,' he replied.

'I'll be down tereckly,' the THING grunted.

Meriweather didn't wait to escort him down. He dropped out of that tree like heavy lead. And he got over behind Gist quick as a greased-lightning flash and lay there a-trembling.

'What is it?' asked Gist.

'There's somebody wants to speak to you,' said Meriweather.

And bam! There was the THING all hunched up before Gist. 'Where's my meat?' it asked in a hollow, growly voice.

Gist like to about died right then and there. He'd never been so scared. He jumped for Meriweather and climbed up him like he was a tree.

'Where's my meat?' the THING repeated, edging closer to the boys.

Gist handed it a piece of meat out of the sack. The THING snatched at the meat and gobbled it down, proper and fast. Gist reached down for another piece. But the THING grabbed the sack and swallowed sack and meat in one belchy gulp.

Meriweather flung it the hide then. The THING crunched up the skull and bones and horns with loud, smacking noises. Then it looked around for more. It poked and snuffled about, and when it could find nothing more, it swelled up in rage.

''Tain't another bit here,' Gist assured it in a quivering voice.

'Then I'll take *you*,' the THING said, slippery-sliding toward him.

'You can't take me,' cried out Gist, backing away, 'for my pa said I had to come home for certain this very night. Take my brother.'

The THING reached out its horrible old claws.

Meriweather leaped behind Gist. 'Take Gist. He's the biggest and much the tenderest,' he sang out. And he tried like everything to push his brother forward.

'I'll just have ye *both*,' snarled the THING, and it leaped toward them.

The brothers lit out of there like rolling thunder, a-running and a-screaming for all they were worth. But their legs just didn't seem to take them away fast enough. And Gist took up a stick and began to beat himself till he tore along wild and giddy and frothing at the mouth like a runaway steed.

Meriweather held on to his brother's flapping shirt tails, and every time Gist hit himself with the stick, Meriweather whacked Gist a good clip with his own stick. Oh, how that did make Gist run!

They came out of the woods with briers and bushy tangles clinging to them and with strips of shagbark hickory curled around their necks and bushels of cockleburs stuck between their toes.

Close behind them came the THING. It crashed through bushes and uprooted trees that had no more sense than to get in the way. It loped along with its big old eyes a-rolling around in its head like red-hot shot and its big old jaws a-slobbering.

The brothers fell in a well and never even stopped there long enough to get wet. They went through haystacks and over mountains and underneath rivers till at last they tired.

'Wait,' said Meriweather. 'All this running will never do.'

Gist agreed. And they thought about disguising themselves as wagon wheels and chimney soot and empty pig troughs. But they didn't know how to do it, so they had to go back to running to escape the THING.

At last Meriweather said he couldn't go another step until he got his breath back. He stopped and leaned against a tree, weak as a jug of town water.

'If you stop now, you'll be eaten sure,' said Gist.

'It don't make me no never-mind,' answered his brother.

And way, way off in the dark they heard the THING holler out:

'Bum, bum, Sally Lum,
Tearing up trees
And throwing them as I come.'

And then there was a crash and a great cracking and splintering of wood.

The two boys didn't wait to hear any more but started off again. They ran and they ran till at last their tongues were hanging down around their knees.

All of a sudden Meriweather stepped in somebody's rabbit snare, and the next thing he knew, he was snatched up in the air by one leg and left dangling upside down.

'Ohhh! It's got me!' screamed Meriweather. 'Help me, Gist! Save me from those terrible sharp old teeth!'

'I'll be back tomorrow to help you,' sang out Gist, and he kept right on going.

But after a while he couldn't resist stopping to watch, for he had never in his life seen a brother eaten up by a THING, and he reckoned it would be a happy occasion.

When he turned around, he saw that Meriweather was caught in a leather noose and was hanging from a bent sapling tree. The THING was not even in sight.

So, Gist came edging back, taking care to keep close to his shadow and being mighty careful to look under every leaf and inside every hornet's nest.

The closer he got to his brother, the more wicked he felt. It wasn't long till he was feeling most powerfully wicked. It set him to quivering all over, and he like to about shook off his breeches.

There his brother was, all caught and helpless as a jar of water on a mantelpiece. Oh, it made him happy just to think about it. He came through the woods grinning. His grin was so wide he couldn't get between the tree trunks, and he had to turn sidewise to pass through.

'Oh, Brother Meriweather,' called Gist at last with a sad shake of the head and a long serious face. 'It looks mighty bad for you, I'll just bid you fare-thee-well quick, for the THING looks powerful hungry to me.'

'Don't let it eat me up, Gist,' whimpered Meriweather. 'Tell the THING I'm double-distilled poison. One bite of me and it'll get rake warts and dropsy, eye sickness and ingrown shrinks.'

'I might just manage to help you, if'n you'll tell Pa it was all your fault we've been out all night,' said Gist.

'I'm to blame,' shouted Meriweather. 'Quick now, get me loose before I'm swallowed whole.'

'And say that I'm the best fighter and can whup you with one hand tied behind me and my eyes tight shut,' said Gist, grinning and enjoying himself greatly.

'Yes, you're the best.'

'Now say . . .' and Gist paused, for he had given out of things he wanted his brother to agree to.

So, Gist reached out and pinched his brother a good hard pinch.

'Oh, help, Gist! The THING is nibbling on me!' shouted Meriweather.

'It's much too late to help you now,' Gist told him. He stooped and got a handful of dirt. 'The THING is shaking salt and pepper all over you so you'll be tasty to eat, Brother Meriweather.'

And Gist flung the dirt over his brother.

Just then a squinch owl hooted its wild quivering cry, and Meriweather knew it as a sure-for-certain sign his death was approaching. Owls never failed to let a body know his time had come. He moaned a little bit. A cloud passed over the moon, and the night was as dark as could be.

'Goodbye, Brother,' called Meriweather. 'I've done been swallowed.'

And Gist lay on the ground and rolled around, laughing and whooping. A moment more and it was light again, and Meriweather saw what was holding him. He loosened the noose about his foot and got down. And he was about to give his brother what-for when there was a loud growl behind him.

There was the THING, bearing down on them like a half-dozen landslides.

> 'Bum, bum, Sally Lum,
> Tearing up trees
> And throwing them as I come.'

Now, the boys were powerful tired of running and being chased. And when they came to a field of watermelons, they jumped in among them.

'I'll lie down here on the ground, and you roll one of them big watermelons on top of me,' said Gist. 'That way I'll be hid real good, and the THING will rush on by.'

'Gladly,' agreed Meriweather, 'but first I'd best stomp you down a little bit all around the edges where you stick up.'

And he kicked and stomped Gist good and hard, for he never liked to miss a chance of doing a good turn of his brother.

But then, try as he would and grunt as he might, he was not able to move a single watermelon. They were just too all-fired big for him to budge. So, Gist jumped up, and they both tried to get one rolling, but the two of them couldn't move it either.

And there came the THING among the watermelons. And it towered up over the boys and pounced.

Now, Meriweather was clever as a barn loft. And the very moment the THING bounded down on them, he took his hunting knife and jabbed it into one of those huge watermelons. And you know, enough juice came squirting out of that melon to wash those two boys away from the THING and over into the next county!

BARBARA IRESON

If you're an eager Beaver reader, perhaps you ought to try some more of our spooky Barbara Ireson titles. They are available in bookshops or they can be ordered directly from us. Just complete the form below and enclose the right amount of money and the books will be sent to you.

☐	CREEPY CREATURES	£1.25
☐	GHOSTLY AND GHASTLY	£1.50
☐	FANTASY TALES	£1.10
☐	GHOSTLY LAUGHTER	£1.25
☐	FEARFULLY FRIGHTENING	£1.25

And if you would like to hear more about Beaver Books in general, don't forget to write and ask for our Beaver Bulletin. Just send a stamped, self-addressed envelope to Beaver Books, Brookmount House, 62-65 Chandos Place, Covent Garden, London WC2N 4NW and we will send you our latest one.

If you would like to order books, please send this form with the money due to:

HAMLYN PAPERBACK CASH SALES, PO BOX 11, FALMOUTH, CORNWALL TR10 9EN.

Send a cheque or postal order, and don't forget to include postage at the following rates: UK: 55p for the first book, 22p for the second, 14p for each additional book; BFPO and Eire: 55p for the first book, 22p for the second, 14p for the next seven books and 8p per book thereafter. Overseas: £1.00 for first book and 25p for each additional book.

NAME...

ADDRESS..

....

Please print clearly